After several years of publishing other people's books Laurence James decided that it was time he started writing some of his own. So, since early in 1973, he has been a full-time freelance author and journalist.

He has had science-fiction short stories published both in Britain and in the United States, but the *Simon Rack* books are his first novels in this field.

His likes include Alf Tupper, Wilson and Braddock as well as old films, old comics and rock 'n' roll. Among many other things he dislikes suits, gherkins and earwigs.

Mr James is married and lives with his wife and three young children in an east Hertfordshire village.

D1634551

Simon Rack

Backflash

LAURENCE JAMES

SPHERE BOOKS LIMITED
30/32 Gray's Inn Road, London WC1X 8JL

First published in Great Britain by Sphere Books Ltd 1975
Copyright © Laurence James 1975

Set in Intertype Granjon

Printed in Great Britain by
Hazell Watson & Viney Ltd
Aylesbury, Bucks

ISBN 0 7221 4981 6

This is for a good writer, a good editor and a good friend. Who else but Ken Bulmer? With a lot of thanks.

ONE

Going Back

There was a hiss of raw power, and the polished wall at his elbow exploded in a glittering blister of molten metal.

'Look out, Simon! This dreck's playing for real.'

The warning wasn't really necessary. When a lab-tech in an advanced weapons establishment went as mad as this one had. Mad enough to kill three guards and get into the ultra-secret armoury. Mad enough to tear the throat out of the boss of the research division with his bare teeth. *And* steal one of the newest hand-guns under the sun – any sun. Then that man wasn't going to be playing for anything but keeps.

Apart from trying to get near enough to the man to waste him with the colt, Simon had the additional problem that he didn't even know exactly what the new gun was or how it operated. Taking a chance, he stuck his head round the corner and shouted : 'Ahmed! Why don't you put it down? Come on. Before anyone gets hurt.'

What he meant was before he got hurt. There were enough bodies scattered bloodily around without adding his own to them.

His shout got little response. Another blast of energy from the gun, and a scream that tailed off into a self-exploratory giggle. Wet and obscene.

Where the hell was Bogart? This wasn't the kind of operation he wanted to face on his own. There needed to be a back-up man with his colt zeroing in on the back of this maniac.

He squinted round the chipped corner of the wall again, in time to see a squat figure blur across the gap between two pillars. There weren't many men in the Galactic Security Service with that sort of figure. Senior Ensign Bogart was doing his stuff.

'You out there! When are you going to come and get me?'

Ahmed! He couldn't have seen Bogart yet. Try and keep him talking. He was in an angle of the building with no escape. Unless you counted the possibility that he might break outwards and get into the wild ravines and escarpments that surrounded the establishment. That was something that Simon didn't want to think too much about. They'd got him bottled up there, and that was the way he wanted it to stay.

'Hey! You all lost your ears, or did I blast your minds with this little lovely?'

Now, was that maybe a clue? Blast minds? That wasn't an idea he liked. Scuttling back round the corner, he pressed the button on his coder. There was the usual crackling of local interference, then he picked up the zonal command.

'Simon Rack. Commander. Trouble at Ad. Weapons. Got a madman with a new gun. I want to know what it is and what it does. Get a double A on that. Out.'

Out of sight, he could hear a muttered, monotone conversation. Every now and again a word or a phrase crept out.

'Blast brains . . . teach . . . laugh at me over . . . she'll not . . . scramble heads and block . . . away.'

At the last word, there was the crack of the weapon, and then the splintering of plas-glass and metal. He didn't need the pattering of feet and the yell to inform him what had happened.

'Simon! He's out!'

There was a door to his rear, and he charged at it, bursting the safety lock with his shoulder. The sky was overcast, with heavy clouds hanging low over the hills to his left. His nostrils puckered at the bitter ammonia smell from the lake that lay a mile or so ahead of him.

8

There was a crackling in the low brush, and he snapped off a hopeful shot with the parax-gun. The power button was three-quarters depressed giving a stun at distance and a probable kill at proximity. The bushes flared as his shot ignited the dry leaves. But there was no cry to show that he'd wounded the fleeing man.

Behind him, there was a thump on the turf as Bogart jumped through the shattered window. Without saying a word – they'd been a team for too long for that to be necessary – Simon waved him round to the left. He ran softly forward, colt at the ready, towards the bluffs overlooking the bitter lake.

It was hot. The temperature had risen above thirty centigrade, and was likely to get even higher as the long afternoon wore on. The shrubs rose eerily about him, towering twenty feet high in places.

Sweat trickled down the inside of his anonymous two-piece uniform, soaking through at the small of his back. He cursed their bad luck at having been around the base when this panic call had come in. They could have been well away, if it hadn't been for an unfortunate misunderstanding with a senior officer about the ethics of snappy saluting.

The caller on his coder buzzed once, and he flicked the switch to bring it to life. All the time his brown eyes roamed around the undergrowth, seeking a clue of movement. There was nothing.

'Yes. Rack here. Go ahead.'

The voice was that of a girl. Cool, efficient, and totally uninvolved. 'Information at twenty-nine, fourteen. The assailant is named Ahmed Sims. Age . . .'

'Cut the dreck, lover. I know about him. I want to know about what he's carrying.'

The voice was slightly less calm and collected. 'Am coming to that, Commander. The weapon is classified.'

There was silence, while he waited for more. There wasn't any more. 'What the hell is that?' he yelped. 'I don't give

9

a flying fart whether it's classified. He's got one, and he's been shooting at me with it.'

'Sorry, Commander.' He could tell from the smug note to her voice that she wasn't at all sorry. 'That's all I can give you.'

With an effort, he mastered his anger. 'Right. Give me a direct link with the research director of this place. And quick!'

There was a momentary delay while circuits whirred and clicked. To Simon Kennedy Rack, it began to seem as though he were alone in a stinking, sweating hell. Moving as quietly as he could, he inched his way through the crackling bushes. At last, ahead of him, he could see light. The end of the undergrowth.

'White here, Commander. You want to know about the weapon Ahmed's taken?'

'Right. And don't tell me it's classified. I know that already. Just tell me what it's supposed to do. And what's its range and rechargeability factor?'

Even as he whispered into the microphone, Simon was still creeping stealthily forwards. The last layer of bushes parted at the touch of his colt barrel and he saw there was a small open space before the sheer drop of the cliff-top. Cautiously, he stepped out on the cropped grass, gun ready in hand, half-crouched for instant movement.

At his ear, the voice of the director gave him the infor-mation he wanted : 'Can't tell you everything, you must understand. But it's an energy-firer. Self-charging. Should last for hours of usage at maximum.'

'Thanks a lot,' thought Simon ruefully.

'Range not more than fifty metres effective, which might help you.'

That was something. While he listened, Simon walked to the edge and looked over, keeping sideways on in case Ahmed suddenly appeared out of the undergrowth. About fifty metres away, he calculated.

It was a fearsome drop. Near enough four hundred metres down, he guessed. Not quite as sheer as he'd thought, but steep enough. Rocks and ledges, all the way down to the placid and deadly lake.

The voice whispered on in his ear :

'Thing is, we're not that sure just what it does do. The only man who really knew is . . . was . . . Levy, and he's gone. Ahmed killed him in the lab. All we had was a clue to what he was doing. We think that he'd stumbled on a memory scrambler.'

'A what?'

'Memory scrambler. Mess up your memory, so you wouldn't know what you were doing. Or why. But there was a lot of lateral power blasting that wrecked everything. He was trying to tighten it up so that the beam would affect the memory and nothing else.'

This had been so amazing and so unexpected that Simon's concentration had briefly slipped away from him. Not the sort of thing a GalSec officer of eleven years' experience ought to do. But he was only human.

There was the wet giggle from behind him and he began to turn, colt swinging in an arc of instant death. But his eyes were quicker, and they told him a story of futility.

The man was at the edge of the vegetation, a grin just hanging loosely on his lips. His eyes were large and staring. A shirt hung loosely off his skinny shoulders, torn in several places. The leap from the window had cost him more than just material, and blood darkened his clothes, threading bright red across his exposed stomach.

The glittering weapon was rock-steady in his right hand, its circular mouth gaping hugely at him. Direct at his face.

The only other thing that his eyes registered, in that split moment of frozen time, was a short man, bursting into view to his right. A colt in his hand. Mouth opened in warning. Eyes opened in horror.

Still Simon kept turning. Knowing that this was one race he'd lost.

Had to happen one day.

To his surprise, he actually saw the stream of energy as it leaped from the barrel of the gun. It arced towards him with an infinite slowness, like a slow-motion nightmare. There was a staggering moment of impact as it hit him flush on the forehead, between the eyes.

There was a time of agonising pain, as though someone had sliced his head apart and was sand-blasting his brain smooth. The filaments of his mind seemed ready to overload and burst.

Bright yellow light exploded through his head, with a hot golden heat. Incuriously, he watched as his hand jerked up his own weapon, spinning it uselessly into the warm, dull air. He noticed his fingers writhing, seeming to claw at space. There was an awareness of travelling backwards, of finding that his feet rested on air.

Of falling. Falling slowly.

Rolling down, through the golden light.

A voice, dimly heard at the edge of awareness, shouting his name.

Falling.

Golden light.

His mind closing down on the present.

Back.

Into the golden light.

Back.

Falling.

Gold. Gold. Gold.

TWO

One Hand Waving

The golden sunlight trickled through the open casement, pouring across the table like a flood of pure colour. It reached over the pile of paper, throwing a shadow as clean as a knife-blade. Beyond the window, the sky hung in an ochre orb over the barren landscape of Zayin. There was not a breath of wind. That came at night. With the cold that shattered rocks and froze the eyes in your head.

The heady scent of the zilax bushes outside seemed to fill the small room, making the thought of report-writing even more of an impossibility. The midshipman off the starship *Venturer* coughed miserably and scratched an insect bite on his wrist. Only four days on Zayin, and a report to write for his Senior Instructor. He flipped dismally through his notes, hoping that they would, somehow, arrange themselves into a semblance of uniformity.

Disjointed phrases leaped at him – culled from a mixture of the *Venturer*'s own vidpix library and his own limited research. Somehow they had to be pulled together to make sense and to convey the past and present of this odd world. 'The usual breathable atmosphere and adequate gravity.' That went without saying. There wouldn't have been an Earth colony in the first place if both those hadn't been within controllable parameters. 'Basic Fed-Eng spoken.' Of course. A legal requirement for membership of the Federation.

What was there that was unusual? The social set-up. The strange splitting into the two extremes. Neither with any real power, yet . . .

'Pssst!'

He looked round. Nobody there. Again, there came the hiss from outside the door.

'Psst! Simon.'

Lilaen! His face broke into a grin. The report could wait just a little longer. Lilaen might not. He shut his notebook with a determined click and got up. He swept through the door and closed it behind him. On the table the sun lay undisturbed across the papers and book. The name on the book was Midman Simon Kennedy Rack – 2987555 – Galactic Security Service.

A day and a half later *Venturer* blasted heavily off the pad at the spaceport of Zayin's main city, Fort Peine. Her massive complement of Federation security officers and men was nearly complete.

'Tell me again, Commander. This Midman, Rack, how long have we had him?'

Fingers rigidly aligned with the non-seam of his uniform trousers, the security commander spoke through clenched teeth. It was a strange habit that he only used when addressing senior officers. They didn't come any more senior than the colonel commanding the *Venturer*.

'Two years, sir. He's nearly eighteen years, sir. Enlisted by guardian off Sol Three at minimum age, fourteen, sir.'

The officer gazed wearily at the file. These young officer-cadets were all the same. Give them a week's leave on a frontier world like Zayin, and half of them went off the rails. The odds were he was dead in a sewer with his throat cut. The picture smiled at him off the three-dee slide in his file. Nice-looking lad. Good training record. Off Sol Three. That was unusual these days.*

---

* For the story behind Simon Rack's enlistment in GalSec see *Earth Lies Sleeping*, also by Laurence James, published by Sphere Books.

'Very well. Mark him "Absent" and inform next of kin. You know the routine, Commander.'

'Sir!' barked the officer, making a quick note in a large black folder he carried.

The colonel looked up, waiting for him to go on. 'Yes? Is young Rack the only one, or is there further bad news?'

'Depends on how you look at it, sir.' The commander permitted himself the rare luxury of a thin smile. 'There is one other absentee, sir. Ensign Eugene Bogart, 2895 . . .'

'. . . 775,' finished the colonel. 'I know his number even better than I know my own. So, he's skipped off again, has he?'

'Sir. Didn't report back from shore leave, sir. Not the first time, sir. Shall I hold his file open, sir?'

'Yes. No point in going through all that again. I wouldn't be surprised to see him turn up again, like a Golot looper. In fact,' he paused as a new thought struck him. 'In fact, Commander, keep them both open. If Rack happens to run into Bogart, that man's damned luck might pull them both through. I remember the time he reported back with that story of the daughter of that minister on . . . where was it? Claimed he had a muscular spasm that lasted eight days and they had to give him a neutronic jolt to get them apart.'

Both officers grinned reminiscently at the memory.

'Yes. Keep both folders open. We're due back in thirty days. Close them if they're not here when we get back.'

The commander clicked his heels and marched to the door of the colonel's quarters, halting at a last thought.

'Or, of course, if we hear they're dead.'

Lilaen had been tempting him ever since he took the room in the house. She was a year or so younger than him, with a rich, warm body that promised more than it ever seemed to give. He'd experienced kissing with the serving girls in the Castle Falcon, and had twice got within touching distance

15

of his goal. But each time something had happened to spoil things, and he resented his long-lasting virginity.

After four years with GalSec, under the strictest discipline in the known galaxies, Simon was beginning to think he'd never manage it. There'd been the usual offers and sly approaches from heshers, for he was a comely boy. He was also nobody's fool.

Now, on Zayin, this was going to be his big chance.

Each time he saw Lilaen, she'd flaunt her body at him, letting him touch at her breasts, bubbling out of a low, tight bodice, or she'd 'accidentally' let her fingers butterfly across the front of his trousers, giggling at the instant response her game got.

He'd tried to get her on her own, but she always claimed she was too busy. There was a red light district in Fort Peine that was off-limits to GalSec personnel, and she had tried, in her turn, to lure him to go with her to one of the drinking places there. A near-dello, called the Red Hole.

'Come on with me there and you can do more than just touch my tits. A lot more. They've got rooms where a man and a woman can enjoy everything.'

She managed to imbue the last word with an almost visible aura of wickedness. Simon felt his loins swell and he itched to get away from his damned report and into bed with her. There'd been the frightening tales of what happened to young cadets who'd gone into drinkers in off-limits areas of frontier planets. They'd been found floating face-down in a stinking river, naked and weaponless.

Simon had seen the training films, and felt sick at some of the ingenious mutilations that he'd seen. It was that alone that held him back from accepting the challenge of the girl.

Anyway, Zayin wasn't really a frontier planet. Not according to what he'd read in the library. There'd been an Earth-based civilisation there for many years. Centuries. Then, things had gone wrong, and there'd been Federation inter-

16

ference to stop a clique of . . . what were they called? Of 'thinkers' – or scientists – taking over for their own ends.

They still existed, these thinkers, but their power was now limited. In all the time he'd been there, Simon had yet to see one of these fabled beings. From all he'd read and heard, they were immensely tall and powerful, striding the planet in some sort of mechanically powered suit.

But they were few in number, and their power had been whittled away to a shade of its former self. Now the planet lay under the benevolent rule of the Federation, and their security service paid a social visit to Fort Peine. Merely to show all men that there was the muscle that backed up the word.

Simon smiled to himself. With a starship and all its crew at the port, it was plain foolishness to think of an officer – a junior officer, perhaps, but a GalSec officer nonetheless – being in danger at an off-limits drinker.

So, when she had come whispering that afternoon, he had gone with her. It wasn't the Zayin winter, when it was death to be out once the sun had plunged down over the horizon in a ball of golden fire. But the nights could still draw chill, and he had wrapped a cloak about his shoulders. There was the reassuring weight of his colt at his right hip, and the coolness of a leaf-bladed throwing knife nestling in a pouch at the back of his neck. Strictly against regulations, but it had been a help in a couple of tight corners.

The girl snuggled her arm through his, pressing her body to him, keeping up a flow of non-stop chatter of the delights that waited at the Red Hole.

The buildings huddled closer as they left the business quarters, and the streets narrowed together. The deep yellow of the sky was fading into dusk as they reached the so-called Crimson Quarter. Here, the old houses had been thrown so closely together in the early days of the colony that they almost met overhead, the roofs nudging each other like a couple of footpads sharing a bawdy tale.

They saw fewer men and women as they hurried on. Most honest citizens of Fort Peine wouldn't dream of showing their faces in the Crimson Quarter at that time of day.

Or at any other time.

Lilaen suddenly pulled him into an alley-way, and his hand dropped instinctively to the butt of his colt. There was the sound of someone walking towards them, along the alley they'd just left. Someone very tall, who walked very slowly.

Simon peered out, feeling the girl tug at the back of his cloak. Half-seen against the darkness, he could just make out a massive figure, towering over two metres tall, striding along with a strange, flowing gait.

'Was that one of. . . . ?'

'The thinkers? Yes. That's why I pulled you back, my sweet little man. We don't want to get mixed up with those old bogies, do we?'

They jostled further into the labyrinth of the old town. Even in his limited experience, it never ceased to amaze young Midman Rack when he visited these planets, to find that there existed the very old and the very new side by side. Zayin had been first colonised many hundreds of years ago, yet the maze of ancient buildings still existed, only a half mile from the newest space port.

And there was still the seething resentment of the thinkers against the arties. They were the creative side of the people's character. Living where they wished, they spent all their time in creating things of beauty, and evolving the moral guidelines for the whole world, from their heavily-guarded centre at Xoachtl.

The arties rarely entered the towns, contenting themselves with remaining in the bare outlands, producing beauty. But Simon had noticed with some interest that there was the barest hint in the research material that they owed something of their creativity to some external agent. What it was remained a secret, but it was suggested that their

18

secret might lie in their fortress, along with all the finest and most valuable art treasures of centuries.

That train of thought had interested Simon, and he'd intended, given more time, to try and get nearer to Xoachtl and see for himself. Even though no outsider had ever managed to penetrate the gates.

At least, nobody had ever lived to boast of it.

Dimly, through the cloaking darkness, Simon saw the red glow of a lamp.

'Is that it?' he asked. Already doubt was running its icy fingers up his back.

Lilaen warmed them away by swinging him to her, and pressing her soft lips against his. 'Yes. That's the Red Hole. Come on. We'll go round the back way.'

She tugged at his arm, swinging him off the alley, knocking him off-balance. Stumbling, he bumped against another figure, bustling through the night, wrapped in a long cloak. Simon was no lightweight, but this man was so vast that he bounced off him like a shuttle in a grav-storm. Both he and the girl crashed against the wall of one of the houses.

'Sorry,' he managed to gasp.

The man turned to face him. Simon couldn't see, but from the tone of the voice it was obvious the man was smiling. 'Don't worry, my dear young sir. I'm better padded than you to take such an outrageous sling. I trust you're not harmed, nor your fine young lady?' He bowed in the general direction of Lilaen.

'No. No, thank you.'

The fat man inclined his head, and strode majestically on towards the drinker.

'Goodness! What with giant thinkers and huge fat giants, this is a real education, Lilaen.'

Slinging her arm round his neck, she pulled him on into a pool of shadow, even thicker than the night. 'Come on. There's a lot more for you to see tonight, love. Isn't there?'

Somehow she managed to entwine herself around him in

such a way that his cloak got all tangled up about his arms, and he could hardly move. Still, it was a pleasant enough imprisonment, and he let her squeeze him tightly.

Quite what happened next, Simon didn't know. There was a rustle of movement, and then the thud of a blow. The crash of someone falling heavily and a groan.

Next, a voice almost in his ear. A voice that he thought he recognised from somewhere.

'Silly boy. Let go the whore and let's move.'

Lilaen gasped and held him all the tighter. 'Who the flame's that? Shag off, stranger, if you know what's good for you!'

The voice chuckled. 'Naughty Lilaen. You don't learn, do you? I did warn you.'

'Nooo!' The voice was a low scream cut off suddenly. The arms round Simon relaxed, and he felt the girl slip to the floor.

Shaking free of his cloak, he pulled out his colt and waved it at the shadow beside him. 'I don't know who you are, but I'd like you to know I'm armed.' He was pleased that his voice didn't seem to shake too much.

'Good boy, Midman. Keep it ready. I fear we might have need of it.'

A light glimmered in the stranger's hand, ranging round the filthy alley. Simon gasped at what the light revealed. The body of a man, blood pouring from a scalp wound, hand still holding a knife. And the figure of Lilaen, equally unconscious, a thin-bladed razor lying limply between her fingers. A black bruise the size of an egg stood out from her forehead.

'Oh,' said Simon. There didn't seem much else to say.

The light flicked up on to his face, pausing. He blinked at it, gesturing with his hand.

'You're Rack. Midman from Four Deck. Cadet from Sol Three. I thought I spotted you by your height. You stand out like a sidewinder in a soya stew here.'

Recognition dawned. 'I know you too. You're Bogart. Ensign Bogart. The one who's always in trouble with Security.'

There was the white gleam of teeth in the darkness.

'Right. Now, boy, we'd better get our asses in gear or the local heavies will have our hides drying on their porches. Come on.'

With good luck, they should have been away from the district and safe back to their quarters.

They had bad luck.

The man on the ground suddenly sat up, and was waving a blaster at them, its wide muzzle gaping in their direction. So fast that Simon didn't even see him do it, Bogart flicked his hand at the man. The sort of irritable gesture that a man might make to wave away a stinging insect.

But, when the light shone on the man he had slumped on his back, and there was the glittering hilt of a knife protruding from his throat. Blood pattered softly on the ground, like a summer shower, threading over the dirty stones.

'God! You've just killed a native. You know what this means, Ensign?'

Bogart was bending over the corpse, pulling the blade free and wiping it on the dead man's jacket. 'Yes, it means that he can't kill us now.'

'But, but what happens now?'

Bogart's voice was still calm and unworried. 'You're supposed to ask me what steps do we take.'

'All right. What steps do we take?'

'Bloody long ones. Come on!'

There was a swirl of movement, and the ensign started to leave the alley. At that moment a window opened at the rear of the Red Hole, sending a bar of clear light across the courtyard.

'Lilaen!' The voice was a sinister hiss. 'Lilaen! Have you finished yet? There's a patrol on the way.'

The girl shook her head and groaned. Bogart hesitated just beyond the reach of the light.

Simon pressed back against the wall, feeling its dampness chill him through his uniform. To his horror, unnoticed by his colleague, he saw that Lilaen had managed to get out a small handgun, and was cocking it, and aiming it at Bogart.

Afterwards, Simon Rack was often asked about the first man he ever killed. Whether he remembered who it was. He did, because it wasn't a man.

There was no time to think about it. The ensign had saved his life, and now . . .

The trigger seemed thick under his index finger, the action of the parax-gun heavy. It was so easy. Easier than he'd ever thought. The stream of death vomited from the colt, steady and true at Lilaen's chest, knocking her back against the wall, hands clutching at herself. The energy locking up the muscles of her heart, paralysing them, stopping the flow of blood in its tracks.

Her mouth opened and no words fell out of her lips. Her eyes opened wider and saw only a dreadful darkness, into which she slid.

'Thanks.'

The one syllable from Bogart, turning to watch the brief scene. A yell came from the man in the window to more of his fellows in the drinker.

Bogart glanced quickly round, looking for a way out of the maze. The labyrinth of courts and lanes would trap anyone not born to them. Already there was an answering shout from somewhere behind them.

'Hunt's up for us, boy. There.'

He pointed to a tilting, shadowed roof, sloping down near to the floor, with a large metal container leaning against it. Simon considered suggesting that they stay and try to explain what had happened. A sizzling bolt from a blaster seared the wall by his arm and changed his mind.

He ran lightly across the stones and hopped up on the

box and then on to the roof. There was a thump as the heavier figure of Bogart joined him. For a moment they were safe. None of their pursuers was yet out of the drinker, and the man who had shot at them from the window would not have seen round the corner to the roof.

Bogart tugged at his arm, and pointed silently upwards, to where a window gaped open. He put his mouth close to his ear and whispered, his lips brushing Simon's cheek. 'There. They'll think we've hopped away and go looking for us. You never look for an escaped prisoner back inside the jail. Come on.'

Before they could climb higher, a mob of armed men boiled out of the Red Hole, shouting and cursing. The yells of anger turned to bitter hatred when they found the two bodies.

'Kill them! Hunt the scum and slash them down!'

Simon held close to the shoulder of the ensign, and hissed: 'Where are the guards? If they come, wouldn't we be better to surrender to them?'

Bogart didn't need to answer. Because at that moment four of the heavily-armed local militia came jingling on to the scene. Clinging to a perilous perch on the roof, they heard the thugs tell the police what had happened. Claiming that two GalSec killers had tried to rape Lilaen and her friend had been killed trying to help her. To cover their tracks, the murderers had slain the girl and run for their lives. There was the chinking of tokens changing hands, and then the crowd evaporated in a surging search, howling for blood, led by the guards.

After they'd gone the courtyard was silent. The two bodies lay where they'd fallen. Bogart sighed his relief. 'That could have been nasty, young Rack. Teach you to go with trollops that want to get their hands on your colt rather than on anything else you might or might not possess.'

Simon found himself feeling faint, and was glad it was too dark for his colleague to see his trembling hands. He even felt as though he might throw up, but that passed. To cover his nervousness, he began to climb silently towards the open window, followed by Bogart.

It opened on to a landing, high in the back of the drinker. To their left was a narrow staircase, winding down towards the bustling ground floor. On the right, the corridor ran in a wide sweep, with doors opening off it. Although they could still hear the noise of shouted conversation from below them, the top of the house was as silent as a midnight tomb.

A strip light gave a pale, watery gleam along the passage, dying in the thick dust on the floor. Wrinkling his lip, Bogart tugged at his trousers, and squatted down on his heels, leaning back against the crumbling wall.

"Right, boy. Let's take stock. Two dead – I did thank you for outing the girl, didn't I? The guards think it was murder. A few chunks of gold'll grease their memories for them. Now, they know we're GalSec, so they'll watch the roads to the port. The Federation's not that popular round here, so they may not even notify them. Just stop us making blast-off and then pick us up when she's safely away. So, we either try and get back, or we stay here and go to earth.'

'Flames of Hell, Ensign! We have to get back. They'll rate us absent.'

'Listen. First, the name's Eugene Bogart. Not "ensign". My friends call me Bogie. Anyone who saves my life automatically becomes my friend, so you call me Bogie. Right? The second thing is not to worry about being late on board. It's happened to me more times than I've eaten fresh eggs, and nothing much to worry about. A few days' extra duties, and maybe some kind of pay deduction. Nothing, boy.'

'If you want me to call you Bogie, Bogie, then you'd better call me Simon. Not "boy". Right?'

'Right.'

There was the sound of feet on a lower staircase, getting louder. Closer.

Despite his shortness and heaviness, Bogart could move

24

like a whisper when he had to. Before Simon had even begun to move, the older man had tried three of the half-dozen doors on the landing. All resisted his hand.

Simon whipped out the parax-gun, depressing the button to give a kill over a narrow beam. With two dead, there wasn't any way back. Bogart tried two more doors, with the same lack of success. But just when it seemed that the men would be upon them, the sixth door swung open.

He beckoned Simon to him, covering his retreat with his own colt. The boy slipped through the open door into the darkness just as the first of the local men appeared round the corner. Bogie slid the door shut, fumbling for the bolt and driving it silently home.

The feet went past, round the next corner, and faded away into silence again. Although there was no light in the room, they were able to see each other. A faint yellow gleam filtered through from under another door. In fact, they saw that they were in a sort of ante-room. From beyond the door, they could just catch the mutter of low-pitched voices.

'It won't be long before those goons outside start wondering whether we're still in here. Then one of them'll cast his red eyes up to that window and that low roof. Then they'll come up here and start looking in all the rooms.'

Simon peered through the gloom at his new friend. 'So what?'

'So there's only one way for us to go, Simon. That's in there.'

His thumb crooked at the closed door.

'There's someone in there.'

'Right. And if they choose to meet in a place like the Red Hole, then they're up to a hell of a lot of no good. That may work for us. Come on.'

Colt in hand, Bogie turned the handle and walked into the room. It was low-ceilinged, with a window – heavily shuttered – on its far wall. A fire glinted in the hearth, sending gouts of brown smoke belching into the room. There were two chairs and a central table. One single light illuminated the chamber with a dark, golden glow. It was just sufficient to see that there were three people in the room.

'Please sit where you are, and place your hands firmly and quickly on top of your heads.'

Simon was right behind him, eyes raking round the small room. There were two men at the table, one seemingly much bigger than the other. The third man was at his elbow, towering nearly to the ceiling. To make him move, Simon rammed the barrel of the colt into his ribs.

To his horror, the man toppled slowly to his right, falling to the floor with a dull crash. For a nightmare moment, Simon thought he was losing his senses, as the creature split into three parts, with the two lanky legs tumbling apart from the trunk and arms.

'Clumsy fool!' squeaked a voice from the other side of the room, where one of the figures at the table was waving his arms angrily. 'You've damaged that and I'll have you ripped apart!'

'Now, now, my dear Fara, I'm sure that our enthusiastic young friend there didn't mean any harm to your precious exo. Did you?'

It was the fat man from the alley-way, standing, leaning his huge hands on the table, the flesh seeming to dribble down his arms and ooze over the wood from his pudgy finger-ends.

'No. It was an accident. I . . .'

Bogie interrupted him sharply. 'Accident or not, my fat friend, you'd do well to sit down and put your hands where you were told. That way my finger won't slip on this trigger.'

Slowly, the big man moved, grunting with the effort of lifting his ham-like arms to shoulder height.

'My dear sir. I admire a man who knows what's what. A man of action after my own heart. But I'd be damnably obliged to know what all this is about.'

Beside him, the tiny figure of a Zayin man sat silent,

eyes fixed balefully on the two intruders. Simon moved to stand beside Bogart, and whispered in his ear: 'What's that?'

'That,' said Bogie in a normal conversational tone, 'is what they call a thinker. One of the old scientist class. They don't like the Federation much, as you'll know if you've done your project properly, Simon. That on the floor is his exo. Without it, he's like a melting jelly in a heatwave.'

'What?'

Keeping a careful eye on the two men at the table, Bogart explained: 'Without that bunch of powered prosthetics, he's like a villain I once knew on . . . where was it? Can't even remember the name. Few years back. Went into medic for an operation for an infected knee. Shooter had got in it and they had to amputate. Unfortunately the doc wasn't on the ball, and he cut off the wrong leg.'

'God! Couldn't he claim against the doctor?'

Bogart grinned wolfishly. 'No. Like our thinker friend here, he hadn't got a leg to stand on.'

THREE

Something's Happening But ...

The golden light cleared for a fraction of time from the brain of twenty-five-year-old Commander Simon Kennedy Rack. His eyes blinked open, and saw an oddly beautiful sight.

Whirling in slow motion about him was a strange, twisting panorama of rock and lake and dull sky. He watched as the sky dipped over his head, then the ground came round and then the smoking liquid of a chemical lake.

At the corner of his vision there seemed to be a man. Or were there two men? Difficult to see properly. There were words as well, but they droned in a slurred bass, like a malfunctioning taper.

Something shiny flicked into sight for a moment, then flicked out again as fast. It could have been the toe of one of his boots.

It really was an extraordinarily enjoyable feeling. Apart from the odd sensation that his brain had come unshipped within his skull and was in free fall at about one-tenth normal time. There was a burning feeling behind the eyes, as though something had hit him.

Something on the edge of pain. Like the beginning of a headache. Briefly, he closed his eyes again, vaguely proud at the ease with which he performed the action.

Immediately, the present rushed away, and he was plunged again into the golden skies of the past. When he was an eighteen-year-old Midman. In a drinker on Zayin. In the stews of Fort Peine.

With a stocky young ensign called Bogart.

'I'd be obliged to know to whom I have the great pleasure of talking.' The voice was soft and calm. The voice of a man totally in control of himself.

'My name's Bogart and this is Rack.'

Despite the threat of the gun, the fat man gestured to rise and shake hands, until the colt made him change his mind. 'An ensign and a fine young midman. Now that's a strange duo to be lurking in a drinker in the back end of Fort Peine. I wonder what on Golot they can be doing. I don't think it can be anything to do with us, my dear Fara, so I suggest you relax and do as they say.'

With a sudden flash of insight, Simon realised that all was not well. Careful and controlled though the fat man was, he was also just that bit on edge. The ragged note at the back of his smooth words was almost invisible. But perception was something that Simon Rack was good at. His psych rating was one of the highest in the recent years of the GalSec trainees.

The fat man was lying. Trying to reassure his Zayin companion not to panic. Why? Because he was worried about what the little thinker might blurt out. So? There must be something worth protecting.

What?

Bogart hadn't answered the man's question. He merely stood watchful and waiting. Simon stepped forward, carefully avoiding the fallen wreckage of the exo-skeleton.

You never got anywhere by standing still. 'What's a rich-looking man like you doing lurking in the back room of a drinker on Zayin, with a thinker? That's also an interesting question.'

'Permit me to introduce myself. As you can see, I'm a man of some wealth. My name is Harley Corman. I'm an agent. That means merely, my young sir, that I will sell my advice on anything to anyone who is prepared to pay me. This respected Zayin citizen is named Fara. He has asked my advice on a personal matter of some delicacy. To ensure our privacy, we arranged to meet here. I trust that we've committed no offence that's going to bring the wrath of the mighty Federation down on our necks.'

The question wasn't even a question. Corman had the best hand and knew it. His first doubts had been reassured. The wheels in his brain had clicked and whirred and come up with only one answer. He had as much right – perhaps a deal more – to be where he was than had the officers. So he could afford the sarcasm.

'Perhaps you lads are in a spot of trouble? We heard some shouting a few minutes ago.' Almost buried beneath rolls of fat, the green eyes glittered with the power of sudden knowledge. 'There were shouts of a killing.'

Simon was not yet experienced enough to completely shelter his feelings from his face. The fat man laughed and slowly lowered his hands. 'Unless you want to add more slaughter to your dirty night out, I suggest you just go your way. Don't worry, we won't betray you. Will we, Fara?'

The tiny figure at the table also lowered his diminutive hands. But made no reply. Bogart and Simon glanced at each other. The lower floors and, for all they knew, all the rooms around were crawling with killers who would be waiting for just one cry.

Bogart's mind moved a little more slowly, and his anger and frustration were less concealed. But he was always a realist. With a sigh he holstered his colt. Simon slowly followed his lead. For a moment the four men looked at each other.

Simon broke the silence. 'Master Corman and Master Fara. The ensign and myself crave your indulgence for our unwarranted intrusion. There has been an accident down below in which we were totally innocent, but the circumstances have been warped to appear otherwise. If you will promise your silence, we will leave now.'

He had moved to stand beside Bogie, and he felt the muscles tensing in the broad body. Casually, he placed his hand on Bogart's shoulder, but his fingers squeezed as hard as he could, trying to prevent any hasty action. To his relief, he felt the older man relax a little.

Corman looked at him, his eyes seeming to burrow beneath the skin of his mind, seeking the truth. Finally, the mouth smiled. 'Very well. You have our word. Master Rack, your path has crossed mine twice tonight. I trust that we will not need to encounter each other again. Such an accident might be an unhappy one for you. Very well. I suggest you get out through this window. There is a ledge outside that will carry you to the right, around the outside of the Red Hole, and eventually to a sloping roof that will cascade you to safety. Farewell. We wish you a safe journey.'

Almost dragging Bogart with him, Simon opened the window, gasping as the freezing air frosted his breath. His feet dangled for a dreadful moment in an abyss of blackness, then they found the narrow ledge. Bogart clambered out beside him.

The huge face of Harley Corman loomed out of the window like a pale, sweating moon, peering at them. Casually, Simon let him see the glint of light on the barrel of a drawn parax-gun. A crescent smile split the face. 'So wise so young will not live long, 'tis said,' he whispered. And closed the window.

The moment the fat man had vanished, Bogart started to argue in an angry whisper. 'You young idiot. You let that load of dripping dreck con us out of that room. Now he's probably screaming down for his mates to come and cut us off.'

Rack felt out and touched him on the chest. 'Quite right. But don't get so worked up. We aren't going the way he said. This ledge has to lead somewhere, so we go to the left. While we're going, you can occupy your mind with what else we could have done. They'd broken no laws. We have – as far as the law here is concerned we're killers. He held all the cards.'

Without a word, Bogie began to edge along the narrow coping, shuffling his feet a few inches at a time. The wind was getting up, and the words that Bogie threw over his shoulder almost vanished in the blackness. But not quite.

'My fucking luck. Fucking one-egg grav! Have to suckle him and try and get us back.'

Simon realised that he was supposed to hear the muttered tirade against himself, and he felt hurt. Maybe he was still young and not very experienced. But . . .

'What the hell else could we have done?'

Over his shoulder, he caught the flash of teeth as Bogie grinned at him. 'Killed them both.'

Simon wasn't sure for some time whether Bogie was really joking or not.

Incidentally, he wasn't.

The ledge threaded round the outside of the drinker, weaving at what seemed a colossal height above the ground. At last, Bogie stopped with a curse.

'What's wrong?'

No answer.

'What's the matter? Why've we stopped?'

'Because the ledge stops. Shut up a minute. There's a window here that I reckon I can open. Yeah!'

Inside they found they were in another winding corridor. On the other side of it there was another row of small square windows. Leaning out of one of them, Bogart was able to see a drainage pipe that wound to the concrete floor below. Suddenly, he pulled his head back in again.

'Armed men. With lights. Going running round the other side of this warren. In the general direction of where we might have been if we'd done what the fat man said.'

After the rushing men had vanished round the corner, Bogie and Simon clambered out of the window and shinned down the pipe. Simon was in such a hurry that he accidentally landed on Bogie's head.

'Suffering Judas! Clumsy prat! Why I have to draw an

innocent like you in this great raffle of life, I do not know. Now we'd better try and get away from here.'

He started to melt into the shadows, then realised that Simon wasn't following him.

'Come on ! Wait here and you're dog meat.'

'The port's that way, Bogie. In the opposite direction.'

Using short words, and speaking slowly – as though he was trying to humour a soft-headed lunatic – Bogie explained.

'They think we're killers. Which we are. So they'll want to catch us to embarrass the Federation. Which it would. So we get caught if we make for the port. Which they'll expect. So we go the other way. Right ?'

'Wrong. If we don't try to get back, then we'll be posted missing. And the *Venturer*'s not due back here for weeks. How do we live till then ?'

Somewhere in the darkness they could hear men's voices shouting orders and contradicting them. The voices seemed to be eddying closer.

'You worry about living for the next few days. I'm more worried for the next few seconds. Come on !'

Bogart dodged off into the night, his colt probing the air in front of him like a sentient limb. Shaking his head at what had happened to him in that one evening, Simon followed him.

Behind them they heard the hiss and crackle of firing and the rising and falling scream of a wounded man, until it was abruptly cut short.

'They've got one of us,' panted Bogart, ducking back into an even narrower alley-way, the concrete walls so close together that they rubbed both shoulders.

Ahead of them a light flicked on, showing they were near a cross passage. Swifter than Simon would have believed possible for such a stumpy man, Bogie pulled both of them into a court that stood open at their side, heaving them down behind a pile of stinking garbage. Face pressed to a supremely obnoxious piece of rubbish, Simon blinked across the slimy stone. The light came closer and paused, not three metres from where they lay. The voices were muted, but still audible.

'They killed Klaus and Terry. Blasted them down when they came out of a window after them. Dirty bastards. Fuck this "hold them for the guards" crap. Kill them both. Hey, what's that? Over there? Come on!'

There was the clattering of studded boots, and the light faded away into blackness. Irritably, Simon pushed off Bogie's hand that had been holding him down in the rubbish. When he spoke, his voice was tight with barely controlled anger.

'Look at me. Best cadet in my whole damned intake. Most promising midman. Bright career in front of me. Commander in a year. And look at me. All in an hour. Now I'm a hunted killer with the chance of missing ship. Lying flat on my face in several inches of muck!'

Bogart chuckled. 'Something in that, my boy. Couple of things I'd like to take you up on, though. Like why your personal file contains so many petty disciplinary charges and the note : "Sometimes seems intractable to orders." And what you were doing anyway with that slut in that dello. But I won't mention any of them.'

In the darkness Simon found himself blushing. He shouldn't have gone with Lilaen, but she seemed . . . And it was true that he hated the petty restrictions of starship discipline. Although the chances of promotion were fewer, he'd almost decided to take the plunge and apply for the lonely duty in the two-seater scouts. The dirty underbelly missions where a big ship and a thousand men weren't that much use. Hearing that his personal file contained so much bad news made him think it would be a good idea to transfer. If he ever got back. And if . . .

'You rotten . . .!'

'Keep your voice quiet. What's the matter?'

34

'How did a villain like you get to see my personal file? I thought that...'

'Only sub-sec commanders and above. Yeah. That's true in a way. Those are the rules. But one thing I've learned about GalSec is that most of their drecky rules are only there to be broken.'

The part of Fort Peine where they lay was creeping back to normal. Silence, broken only by distant shoutings. Quietly both men got to their feet, and wiped the worst of the garbage off themselves.

'Now?'

Bogart looked around them. In front of them the massive labyrinth of Fort Peine stretched out, its bigger buildings several storeys high. Behind them lay the barren wastes of the outlands.

'That way,' Bogart said, pointing to the front, 'is the city and the spaceport. A chance of safety and a probability of death. Whereas, that way,' he said, pointing round behind them, 'is a baking desert, with a few artie colonies and a hell of a lot of nothing. Almost certain death.'

All the conditioning of GalSec had drilled obedience to the core of Simon Rack's soul. Well, nearly to the soul. Right at the centre there was a small room that couldn't be entered. There the conditioning didn't reach. There he was his own man; and always would be.

'Come on. What's it going to be?'

'Hell! I never liked starships that much, anyway. Let's go and look at the backlands.'

'Don't worry. There is water there. But they classify them as just deserts.'

Simon laughed. 'That's what they said I'd always get. My just deserts.'

Dawn found them several miles out of Fort Peine, on the edge of the backlands. A cave, hollowed out by one of the

35

earlier settlers centuries ago, served them for a shelter.

'I don't see why this place died, Simon.'

That was an easy one. His research had been thorough until Lilaen had interfered with his studies.

'Zayin was once one of the potentially great planets on the border fringe of the early Federation. There were hopes that it could become one of the great galactic pleasure grounds. Unfortunately there were fearful internal political problems. You can see what's left of them in the hostility between the thinkers and the arties. It came at a crucial stage in the planet's development, when the Shuckburgh Scale lay at the expansion figure. So nobody came after all. And since then figures have gone down.'

'They held a population explosion and nobody turned up.'

'Well, you could put it like that. If you're flippantly minded you could. Anyway, now there's still the arties with a secret fortress somewhere in the backlands, and there's a few of those thinkers, still trying to work out ways of getting back a bit of power for themselves. All on a dying world, and all for nothing. Shame.'

While they were talking, the golden dawn had come up like molten thunder, stippling the rough-hewn walls of the cavern with yellow dust. Far, far overhead the shadowy ring of space detritus – known as 'Zayin's Halo' – hung in the sky like a vast Gothic arch, staining the pure ochre of the dazzling firmament.

Simon crawled to the lip of the cave and peered out, shading his eyes at the unexpected brightness of the morning. The landscape stretched out far before him. The sandy-stone cliffs and buttes and mesas rolled out before him, their hugeness making it difficult to judge any distances.

'Reminds me of some place in one of the old vid-films. From way, way back. Settlers versus Redskins. One of those. About a wagon full of folks trekking across a land just like this. A valley full of monstrous monuments of rock. By a man called . . . can't remember. But they named an automobile after him.'

Bogart crawled out to join him, also rubbing his eyes at the golden dawning.

'Judas' blood! Look at that sky. You don't really dig it in that slum back there. What a big mother of a rising sun. But there's still a nip in the air!' He shivered.

Simon had no food or drink of any kind, but Bogie had brought along his survival kit. 'Always do, my boy. Never know when you might need it. Remember that. Here, have a con-cap. Delicious. Add inches to your height. Not that you need any inches. You look like an extruded piston as it is.'

Simon grinned. It was true that he topped the older man by several inches. But he'd been born in the normal gravity of Sol Three, while Bogie had been born in the tough colony of Marsbase. The gravity there, despite all the efforts of the scientists to artificially decrease it, was still heavier than most Federation planets. Therefore, Bogart was short and squat. And powerfully muscled.

'Better than looking like a reject fuelling carton.'

Both men thoughtfully munched on the tiny pill. It was supposed to give them the equivalent of two and a half thousand calories.

It did.

It also tasted like processed mud.

After their banquet both men went discreetly and separately to the rear of the cave to perform their evacuatory processes. Accompanied by the usual coarse jokes. Bogart went second, and had just finished zipping up his two-piece uniform when they heard a high-pitched whine.

'What the . . .?' Simon went to the mouth of the cavern, peering out across the deserted land.

'Get your ass back inside!'

'Why?' But he did move back into the shadow.

Bogart joined him, taking care not to move into the pool of golden light just outside the mouth.

'That's a copter of some sort. Maybe a Keeta Five. They've still got some of those around here. Saw one at the port when we came in.'

'You think they're out looking for us?' There was a note of disbelief in Simon's voice. 'They can't think we're that important. Maybe it's a team from the ship looking for us.'

The whining grew louder, but the ship – whatever it was – remained out of sight, somewhere up and behind them.

'Listen, Simon. Midman Rack. There will not be a team from the *Venturer*. They never ever chase defaulters. The reward for turning them in makes sure they don't need to. No. It must still be that damned killing last night. But,' his voice grew puzzled, 'I'd always heard that the law here on Zayin wasn't exactly famous for chasing criminals. So why all this hassle over a dello drab?'

The wheels that had been clicking around in Simon's head finally meshed. 'Wait a minute. The fat man. I knew his name rang a bell. Harley Corman. Remember the assassination of the princeling on . . . where was it? Yes, on Reimak. That nasty toy that blew up in his face. There was a very fat man on the platform with him in some of the vid-shots. I noticed him just because he was so gross.'

Bogart looked at him, knowledge dawning slowly over his craggy face. 'Wait a minute, son. A very fat man. I recall . . . before your time it would be . . . Holy Hannah! You're right on the beam, boy. Harley Corman. The royal jewels went missing from Metela Two. Or Three. Doesn't matter. Man claiming to be a Federation agent had called to check them out. He was a very fat man. Well, well, well.'

Suddenly, the whine grew to a roar, and the fine dust below the cave's mouth swirled and danced as a silver copter swung overhead. It was polished and narrow, like a flying hypodermic, a quester in its nose searching and peering. Although they knew it wouldn't pick them up in the shadow of the rocky overhang, both men pulled back a couple of steps.

To their amazement, the first copter was followed by another. And then a third. All wheeling slowly across that red desert towards the east.

In a ravine about a mile away, a small, four-legged marsupial darted for cover, frightened by the din of the machines. The nearest of the ships swung lower and a beam of glowing energy cracked out. It hit the little animal in the chest, bowling it over and over. A red spray of burst intestines splashed over the rocks.

Neither officer spoke as the ships slowly vanished in the distance, quartering the ground in their lethal patrol. At last their glittering shapes disappeared into the golden haze.

Bogart let his breath out in a loud snort.

'So! Team-handed just for us. Someone somewhere really wants us found. What do you reckon, Simon?'

Rack sat down, leaning his back against a wall of rock. To occupy his hands while he talked, he started to field-strip and wipe clean his parax-gun. 'Look at the facts, Bogie. One. We were responsible for at least one death. Yes, I know they were out to kill us, but I'm looking at it objectively. Two. We ran into one of these little thinkers. Closeted away in a dark room with someone that we both now think is one of the biggest villains in the galaxy.'

'In any damned galaxy, from what I remember. Sorry, Simon. Go on.'

'Right. Three. We get chased by every security ship in Fort Peine. Right out here, in the backlands. It all hangs together.'

Bogart's face crumpled with the effort of trying to follow a lengthy train of thought. 'They must be linked?'

'Yes. Of course they are. Corman's used some kind of pull – probably big bribes – to get us hunted down.' Another thought suddenly occurred to him, and he stopped his absent-minded polishing. 'Judas! They aren't trying to take us in, Bogie. They're out to blast us into the sand. So, we reach four. We must have interrupted something important.'

'Between Corman and the thinker?'

For the first time, but by no means the last time, Simon was amazed how a man who could react to danger as fast as Bogie did could also have such painfully slow thought processes when it came to ideas.

'Yes. Now, what could someone like Corman be up to with a thinker? You reckon they might be going to try to take back some of their power from the arties, and they want to use Corman as a killer for them? That could just be it. Hell! We've got to tell *Venturer*. I'll call her up on the talkie coder and tell them.'

He put his colt back in its holster, and fumbled round behind him for the neat oblong box of the coder. As he did so, he was vaguely aware of the high whining of the copters, stabbing across the warm air.

The familiar buttons and tiny dials glittered in the golden light. He set the pattern for the main communications channel of the starship, ready to press the call switch. A large muscular hand clamped across his, holding him still.

'Think, boy. Before you do something as stupid as calling up *Venturer*. Think.'

By now the whine had become a roar. Safe inside their cave, they peered cautiously out, watching the slim ships quartering the area around the rocks. Every now and again there would be the crack of the guns as something moved in the desert. Or seemed to move. It was obvious that the men were firing at anything, regardless of what or who. Without any warning, one of the copters blasted at the entrance of their cave.

There was the hiss of raw power, and both men ducked as blackened splinters of rock cracked about their ears. Smoke, tinted pink by the violent ionisation, drifted round them, making them both cough. Chunks of the roof of the opening crashed down, half-closing their way out. But, there was still enough of a gap to climb out. Neither man moved until the engine noise had faded away to a drone.

'They aren't playing games, are they?'

'What do you think'll happen once you press that call switch? Eh?'

Simon was unable to check a pink flush rising above his collar. His voice was low. 'They'd pick it up as well,' he muttered. 'They'd zero in on us just like that. I'm sorry, Bogie.'

The face crumpled up, this time into a broad grin. 'Listen, Simon. I don't mind working with someone who makes an occasional mistake. Anyone can do that. What I hate is having to work with some useless load of dreck that makes the same mistake twice. You can't afford that sort of thing.'

Simon clambered forwards, scratching his knee on the razor-edged shards of rock. He reached the pile that had been blasted from the opening, and peered over it. 'We can get out easily,' he called. 'Maybe we can use the coders when they're right out of sight.'

Bogart noisily sucked at his front teeth. 'I thought you midmen were supposed to gen up on planets you visited?'

'Oh, no. What've I said now?' asked Simon, swinging round to face Bogart. 'Why can't we do that?'

Panting with mock-exhaustion, Bogart scrambled up to join him on top of the rock-fall. Shading his eyes, he stared across the broken land, the glare of the golden sun fragmenting off the red boulders.

'You've been to Sol Six?'

'Is that Saturn? No. Been past it.'

'What's it famous for?'

'The rings around it.'

'Right. What effect do they have on communications?'

Simon saw the light. 'Oh. Of course. They scramble everything. That's why it's not settled properly.'

Bogart pointed up into the clear sky. 'And what's that up there?'

It wasn't necessary to reply. The sky of Zayin had one other distinctive feature apart from its rich ochre hue. High over the planet, a little beyond its atmospheric layer, was an arc of shadow. Composed partly of the shattered remnants of an age-old satellite, the Ring of Zayin had also attracted a deal of space detritus. Asteroids circled in it, as did the wrecks of several ships, covering centuries of design.

Apart from casting its bridge of darkness over the world, the ring also acted the same way as those of Saturn, by blocking out any form of communication for long periods of time.

'In any case, Simon, *Venturer*'s due to lift-off very soon. We'll probably even see her go over. But, apart from watching her there's damn-all we can do. No, I'm afraid we're on our own.'

At last the sound of the searchers faded away to nothing, and the two men were able to climb out into the open again. By now the temperature had risen to a degree that caused some discomfort. Bogart ripped open the front of his uniform, and Simon followed suit. After all the damage they'd suffered the previous night, one more tear wouldn't do that much harm.

Somewhere away behind them, in the direction of Fort Peine, there was the familiar rumble of a massive pheronium-drive motor warming up, ready to lift off a starship.

'*Venturer*?'

Bogart nodded. 'Has to be. There weren't any other starships at the port. Yes. Here the old cow comes.'

The description was grossly unfair. The *Venturer*, like all the biggest Federation ships, was a thing of beauty. Vast – more unimaginably huge than the eye could comprehend – with enough space to carry a crew of hundreds and up to a couple of thousand troops.

They were the principal tools of the GalSec branch of the Federation. One could subdue a city, and five could crush a world. They were not the most sophisticated weapons, but they formed an almost irresistible striking

42

force. Their strength was also their weakness. They could put down an armed rebellion but they were useless for a small operation.

The intricate and delicate balance of power in many of the Federation planets sometimes demanded a more delicate weapon. That was where the small two-man scouts came into their own. And that was where Simon Rack wanted his career to take him. To the undercover missions. Missions where two men might succeed where a thousand would fail.*

But, right now it seemed as though his career might have ended before it had even begun.

He waited at the foot of the mesa and Bogart scrambled to the top and peered back towards the city. While he was up there, the distant rumble deepened, and the air shook with the shock-waves. There was the glint of gold light rising faster and faster into the air. Then the noise melted away and the silence scampered back again.

The *Venturer* had gone.

Ever since he could remember, Simon had scarcely ever been so isolated. As a boy there had always been the company of other lads, and once he was joined to GalSec the word 'privacy' ceased to exist. There were always other cadets and, later, other midmen around him. The starship had wrapped itself around him like a huge armoured womb. Now that had been untimely ripped from him and he felt the chill.

He shivered despite the excessive heat and humidity. A clattering of pebbles and sliding rock above him reminded him that he was lucky enough to have a comrade. And not just any comrade either. A man who'd become a legend in his own brief lifetime in GalSec for a mixture of brilliance in action and gross insubordination when not in action.

Bogart's voice floated down to where he stood waiting. 'Simon! Bad news, boy.'

'What is it?' He started to climb up the face of the

* See *Simon Rack: Earth Lies Sleeping.*

mountain to see for himself, when another shout from Bogie halted him.

'Wait there! I'm coming down. There's something coming out of Fort Peine, and it's headed this way. There's the biggest damn cloud of dust you ever did see. I just figure that it might be for us.'

Once again rocks and stones clattered down the eroded sides of the mesa, only this time they were followed by Bogie. He slid so fast that he rocketed past Simon, collapsing in a heap of rubble at the bottom.

Simon slid down to join him, helping him to his feet. 'Are you all right, Bogie?'

A bout of coughing and spluttering answered him. 'Ooh! Sod it all! That bloody Corman! You and I have a lot to do, young Simon. That way,' he said, pointing towards the baked areas of the backlands, 'means a quick death from lack of water and heat. But that way,' he said, pointing behind them, towards the city, 'is a load of men who are not going to be friendly.'

'So?'

Gathering his breath again, Bogie dusted off his uniform. 'I had an instructor in personal combat, who once said that if there were fifty men with blasters in front of you and forty-nine men with blasters behind you, then you tried your luck with the forty-nine. In other words, use all the odds there are. So, we go on. Come on.'

'But, Bogie, where? Where are we going?'

The only answer was a finger, pointing out into the shimmering distance.

'Judas! I hate getting sand in my boots.'

Bogie laughed. 'Never mind, Simon. Smash this fearful conspiracy and all will be forgiven.'

'I still hate sand in my boots.'

'Remember what old Commander Wayne used to say. "Show us your true grit." Let's go.'

'The desert areas of Zayin, known as the backlands, are a wild and greatly eroded region, with little wildlife and less water. Apart from the few settlements near the fringes – of which Fort Peine is easily the largest – the backlands are minimally populated. The so-called "arties" are thought to have some forms of habitation in the desert areas, but they are of a nomadic type. NOTE : It is also claimed that the arties have a fortress of some kind in the backlands. No Federation operative nor any normal citizen of Zayin has ever located it. But there have been too many unexplained disappearances in the region to be simply marked away as accidents. The fortress, according to legend, contains great wealth, hidden and guarded somewhere near Xoachtl. Also, though this is mainly supposition, it is claimed that a mysterious source of the arties' talents also lies buried within this desert stronghold. It is to be avoided at all costs by Federation personnel. Contravention of this regulation will be punished most severely.' Galactic Security Service Infosheet No. ZG 870164 (Zayin).

It had not been a good day. Although they never saw their pursuers, there was a constant cloud of dust rising in an orange column behind them, nibbling at their heels. The rocks cut at their boots, and both of them had cuts and grazes from falls. The golden sun roasted the land, making the glassy boulders too hot to touch with the bare skin.

Only towards evening did they finally see their pursuers falling away behind them. Four times they had been forced to shelter by copters flying low overhead, firing indiscriminately at any hollow or cave.

Simon was in worse shape than Bogart. His face was flame-red and skin already peeled off his nose and forehead. Although they'd tried to improvise some kind of shelter from the sun, their uniforms gave them little material to work with, and their caps lay many miles behind in the red-light district of the city.

Sweat still ran from every pore of their bodies, soaking blackly into their clothes, and evaporating wastefully in the hot air. Simon's tongue felt twice too big for his mouth, and his lips were like swollen pieces of raw leather.

When he tried to talk, his voice cracked, coming and going. He coughed and swallowed, trying to bring some little moisture to his mouth. 'Bogie, can't we take a couple of aychers?'

'Listen, Simon. Those water tablets have to last us days. Maybe weeks. One at night, after the sun goes down, and one in the morning before we start walking again.'

Simon collapsed to the ground, tucking himself into the lee of a large rock. The shade gave him an illusion of coolness. He tugged off his boots, and shook out tiny splinters of rock and crystalline sand. The thin socks on both feet were torn and dark with blood.

'Bogie. We've walked all day. We've got rid of the hunters for a bit. We haven't seen one of those frigging shiny copters for hours now.'

The ensign squatted on his heels by his side, grinning mirthlessly through the burned mask of his face. 'Right, Simon. Right on every count. What's the next question?'

Simon closed his eyes, rubbing at them with the back of his hand. Although it hurt to rub them, it somehow didn't seem as bad as having the constant irritation of hot sand grating at them. Finally, he stopped and peered up at Bogart through the range of cartwheeling colours. As he stopped rubbing, so the colours quickly faded.

'Where?'

Eugene Bogart stood up, groaning with the effort. 'Listen to me, Midman Rack. We have reason to suspect that Corman is up to no good with the thinkers. Right? So, the ones most likely to suffer from that could be the arties. Right? We can't go back to Fort Peine. We can't strike south towards Fort Dure. They'll have our idents by now. The only way is out. But I reckon we've gone far enough for today. We'll camp for the night in that ravine over there.'

Normally, if the men had been on active service, they would have carried full field survival packs. But Bogie had been having a night out, and Simon had nearly done something he'd wanted to do for a very long time. So, neither of them were prepared for a hard march across some of the most hostile terrain in the known universe.

Each man carried his colt. Bogie wore a thin-bladed knife at the back of his belt, and had been approving of Simon's dagger. Though both were contrary to GalSec ordinances. Each of them carried a bare essential of food and drink tablets in his belt pouch, but they were only designed to take a man through a few days. Neither knew how long those days would be, and they shepherded them carefully. Apart from that, and their coders, they were totally unprepared.

Simon was lying down, trying to adjust the contours of his body to the harsh angles of the rocks beneath him, when he was conscious of movement. A body was wriggling up against him, pressing closer. He barely restrained a yell, and kicked out. There was the satisfaction of feeling his boot dig into flesh, and he heard someone groan.

'Bogie? There's someone here. I got him.' His hiss produced no instant reply. Just a louder groan.

Then : 'You sodding stupid bastard ! What the fuck are you playing at? Eh?' There was a long drawn-out moan, and the sound of someone rubbing themselves. 'It was me. Silly sod !'

Simon couldn't really think of anything to say. 'My God, Bogie, I'm ever so sorry. I just thought . . .'

'That I was a vicious, marauding thinker.'

'That, or . . .'

'Or, what?'

'Well. I know that some starships have quite a few . . . you know . . . heshers.'

47

The snort of laughter was so loud that Simon wondered if there were any of their pursuers in the area.

'Heshers!' The laughter was checked by another groan. 'God, you've got hard feet, young Simon. But, no. I'm not a hesher. Not by any manner of ways. That's one thing I've never been worried by. Quite the obfusc, so to speak.'

Simon found himself shivering with the cold. Then he realised. 'Hell! Because of . . . so we could both keep warm. I'm sorry, Bogie. Come on.'

So, the night passed slowly, with both men huddled up to each other, each waking if one moved, waiting for the first glinting of the warm sun.

When it finally rose, Bogart stretched stiffly and groaned to his feet. 'I'm going up that butte to have a scout round. If you see or hear anything, just whistle. You do know how to do that, don't you? Right. See you.'

His boots sliding in the sand, he clambered off up the steep face. Simon nibbled a food tablet and looked around him. The maps of Zayin, despite the number of years that it had been colonised, still showed vast blank areas. Mainly because it had never been worth anyone's while to chart the huge interior backlands. There were no valuable minerals, and nothing grew there.

From what he could remember, there was only one thing anywhere out where they were headed – the almost mythical fortress centre of the arties, called Xoachtl. But none but the elect of the arties knew where it was. That was, if it really existed at all.

There were tales of men staggering back to Fort Peine with madness in their eyes and froth on their cracked lips. Men who died in raving fits, babbling of the beauties of Xoachtl. Claiming that they'd found it, but that something had blasted the sense from their minds. Incapable of ever telling where it was. But it must be there somewhere. It had to be.

Simon was abruptly conscious of being watched. Slowly,

letting his eyes move first, he swung round. The hair rose silently at the nape of his neck, and he swallowed hard. Despite being dehydrated by the desert, he felt the palms of his hands grow slick with sweat. His tongue felt too big for his dry mouth.

Facing him, barely twenty metres away, crouched a tawny animal. Roughly the size of the striped felines he had seen pictures of on Sol Three. Nearly three metres long, with four lethally-clawed legs. A head with a thick mane, and a mouth equipped with three rows of yellow teeth.

A phrase from the GalSec guide to Zayin crept to Simon's mind. 'The khetam was the most voracious and fierce creature that inhabited the backlands. Although it is deemed possible that there are still a few of these animals alive, they are doubtless in poor condition and will present little threat to the wary traveller.'

'You can deem that again,' muttered Simon to himself.

The khetam pulled its lips back off its teeth and snarled at him. Its stubby tail whipped to and fro, stirring up the light dust. Slowly, one foot in front of the other, it started to advance on him. Keeping his own movements as gentle as possible to avoid provoking the beast into a mad rush, Simon eased the colt from its holster, depressed the button on the grip to full, aimed and fired.

Nothing.

The bolt of stunning energy that he'd expected didn't happen. Not even the whirr of the power cell charging. The khetam hissed its anger and suddenly charged.

There wasn't time to draw the leaf-bladed throwing knife from behind his neck. Not that it would have been a deal of use against a creature of that size and ferocity. All he could do was duck and yell.

The charge took the khetam clean over his head, though one of the powerful back paws hooked down at his shoulder, barely grazing the material of his uniform. He rolled over and swung back to his feet. The khetam had checked and was again watching him. Its eyes stared, red-rimmed, with a golden iris at the centre. Simon noticed that the sun glinted off the flecks of sand on its pelt.

He shouted for Bogart, but his colleague was somewhere out of sight. The beast coughed, hacking up lumps of green froth hanging from the whiskers round its angular jaws. The eyes narrowed, and it squatted back on its hind legs, tensing its body like a tightly-coiled spring. Simon eased his knife from its leather sheath, and balanced it on the palm of his hand.

There was the hiss of breath, and the khetam was on him. But, at the last minute, it changed course, and dodged to the side. He spun round to face it, ready for its next trick.

'True what they say. Never trust a khetam!' he said quietly.

This time the spring was for real. If anyone had been watching out there in that desolate waste, he would have seen an extraordinary sight. As the big cat sprang, Simon Rack dived *forwards*! Towards the beast.

But his dive carried him under it, and he rolled and was on his feet again before the infuriated animal had readied itself for another leap. The knife whirred from his fingers, spinning towards its target. The khetam saw it coming, and dabbed a huge paw at it. Too slowly and too late.

The tiny blade thunked home right in the centre of the creature's left eye, sticking there like some bizarre ornament. Clear fluid jetted out, tinted pale yellow. The liquid splashed softly on the rocks, leaving a dark trail over the dryness.

The khetam screeched its agony and shook its head furiously, trying to dislodge the knife. But it was firmly wedged. The roars filled the ravine, deafening Simon. He'd made his play, and all he could now do was stand and watch.

Blood flowed over the animal's face, and it coughed and snarled. Suddenly it stopped and stood quite still, watching Simon. Slowly it sank back on its haunches, then rolled over on its side. Its paws clawed at the air, and a low moan came from its throat. The huge head shook once as though in bewilderment, then it died.

With impeccable timing, Bogie chose that moment to come sliding round the face of the bluff, his colt ready in his hand. He took the scene in at once, and holstered the gun.

'Whew! Sorry I took so long, but I was climbing on a tricky bit. Came as fast as I could.' He walked forward and peered at the knife, tugging it free from the creature's eye, and wiping it on the tawny fur. Already the tiny winged predators were humming and buzzing about the corpse, lapping at the trickle of blood.

'Right in the eye and right through to the brain.' He wiped sweat from his face. 'Jesus H.! That's not bad, young Simon. Not bloody bad at all. You must practise a lot.'

Simon grinned. To his surprise, he found that his fingers were trembling slightly as he took the blade back from Bogie and fumbled it into the sheath behind the neck.

'A little,' he said drily.

During his climb Bogart had seen a smudge of what looked like smoke far away to the north. Further into the desert. That was the way they began to walk, picking their way carefully over the splintered rocks. Simon checked his useless colt but found nothing obviously wrong with it. Regretfully, he rammed it back in the greased holster.

At the top of the canyon, they paused and looked back at the scene of the encounter. A cloud of flies almost hid the body, hanging like a swirling pall of smoke.

'You know someone once told me that they used to export the khetam's paws.'

Simon looked at Bogie in puzzlement. 'Its paws! What the hell for?'

'Eating.'

'You're joking me, Bogie.'

'No. Truly. They were a special delicacy in those high-class joints that serve that stringy dreck. Pasta. That's it. Pasta and khetam.'

Far above them, the sun rolled behind the arc of detritus that hung over the parched face of Zayin.

Simon clapped Bogart on the shoulder. 'Come on. If we're going to get to that smoke.' He paused, taking a final look back down the canyon. 'But I'll tell you one thing about that khetam. He may have had a pasta, but he's surely got no futura.'

Laughing, they walked off to the north.

FOUR

Enjoy the Trip?

With the clarity of cool, fresh water after days of recycled bodily liquids, Simon Rack suddenly became aware that he was, in all probability, about to die. Despite the effect of the mind-blaster, with its weird slowing of time, part of his brain continued to function with a sort of normality.

He took a slow, deep breath, feeling the bitterness of the biting ammonia. It was impossible to focus his eyes properly, but he guessed that he must be falling at a normal rate, while his mind, affected by the new weapon, told him he was moving in tenth-time.

There was a crashing blow to the back of the head, as he rolled over a rocky outcrop. Followed swiftly by a crack to the right knee, bringing a muffled, distorted groan of pain from Simon.

The agony was so intense that he wished he could scream, but something seemed to be holding back the noise.

The agony was so intense that he wished he could scream, but something seemed to be holding back the noise.

At last, he managed to croak out a curse. 'Golot's tombs ! ! Bogie, this can't go on. I'm dying of thirst. The bloody golden light's got to my eyes and I can't see where we're going. This rock is worse than fused levium to walk on. One more fall like that and you can boil my kneecaps for sauce. My boots are falling apart. In other words . . .'

'In other words, you aren't happy in your work. What did you expect? Did you believe all that prop crap about it being a man's life with GalSec? Patrolling the skyways.

Keeping the stars free. Come on. You may only be an eighteen-year-old midman, but you don't have to give up that easily. Come on, only another few miles and we're there.'

Bending and stretching his leg, wiping off the smear of blood from the last painful fall, Simon grinned at him. Even that was painful, with cracked and sore lips, but he managed it. 'All right, you s.o.b., you don't have to go on. I could walk you into the floor any day. I reckon that my legs would only be worn halfway down, and yours'd be bleeding stumps.'

The day was nearly done. The sun had travelled across the ochre sky, and was now sinking behind the mountains to the north. The mountains where Bogie claimed to have seen smoke.

Both men were feeling the strain. Even Bogie's iron constitution was fraying at the edges. Their uniforms were in tatters and their boots worn through. Simon's mouth was a mass of cracked sores, his tongue filling his dry mouth like a chunk of salted meat.

'There !'

'Where ?'

'There. Triangular peak, twenty . . . twenty-two degrees right and about forty down. See it ?'

'Got it. Looks like a watch fire of some kind. That must have been the smoke I saw earlier in the day. Look . . .' Bogart shaded his eyes against the setting sun. 'Up there against the cliff. Those round balls. What the hell are they ?'

Simon peered into the distance. There seemed to be clusters of round objects, stuck to the walls of the cliff, above the place where the smoke spiralled upwards. In the medical for acceptance to GalSec, Simon had recorded ninety-eight/ninety-nine vision. That wasn't perfect. But it was the highest of any candidate for entrance in the previous sixteen years.

'They're all different colours. Can't see any more. It's

a bit far to pick out any people. Maybe they're some kind of habitation. I reckon that . . .' He stopped suddenly.

'What's the matter, Simon?'

'Well. I could have sworn that one of them just moved across the wall. Couldn't have been. Could it?'

Cautiously, reckoning that where there was fire there must be men, Bogie and Rack clambered across the arid land. They stopped at the rim of a huge crater, at least three miles across. It was all that separated them from their objective. They lay together and looked across. The needle of orange light could be seen more clearly, but the houses – if that was what they were – had faded away into the swooping blackness of night.

Bogie spat down disgustedly into the crater. 'Judas! Look at that. It's worse than anything we've crossed so far. What a frigging place. Like the devil's ass-hole. Still, we're close to it now. Whatever it is.'

'Hey!' To Simon's embarrassment, his voice gave an unexpected upwards trill. It had broken two years ago, but there was still this occasional falsetto squeak that betrayed his youth. 'Maybe it *is* Xoachtl. Maybe that's it over there. Maybe it does exist. Maybe we can find the arties there and they'll help us. Maybe . . .'

Bogie laughed. 'Maybe, maybe, maybe. You sound like one of those old pre-neut singers. Holly his name was.'

But Simon wasn't to be sidetracked. 'Never heard of him. Anyway, it could be. Couldn't it?'

Bogie grinned. 'Oh boy! Listen to me, Simon. You can rave on all you like, but just think it over. It's so easy to jump to conclusions, but Xoachtl! With all that gold. That'll be the day.' And he laughed again, as though he'd just made some very clever jokes.

Simon looked at him in bewilderment. 'What the hell are you laughing at?'

'Oh, it doesn't matter any more.'

Despite the darkness and the splintered rocks everywhere underfoot, they both agreed to press on during the night to try and make it to the arties' camp. Or whatever it was. There had to be food there, and precious drink.

The only light came from the dim glow from the Ring of Zayin, throwing the faintest of shadows off the needled landscape. Gradually, painfully, and relatively silently, they neared their objective.

The flame from the fires grew brighter, and they could make out the figures of men and women moving round them. Bogie had wanted to attract their attention before they got too close, but Simon had urged caution.

At last, hands bleeding, they reached the bottom of the crater and began the careful crossing of its tortuous rocks. They were just over halfway over when Bogie suddenly began to hum to himself. The tune was an old GalSec ballad about the improbable mating of a colonist and a female lizard, containing several permutations that were not only obscene but totally impossible.

At another time Simon would probably have joined in, but now he was horrified that his partner should make so much noise at such a time.

'Shut up !' he whispered.

The humming merely grew louder.

'Bogie ! What the hell are you up to? They'll hear us.'

In fact, they were still sufficiently far away from the group of people for that sort of noise to go undetected. But there was no way of knowing whether the men had sentries out.

'But when she took hold of his trusty old colt . . .' Now there were words as well as humming.

Without any warning Simon began to feel nauseous, though he'd had little enough to eat. At the same time his irritation with Bogart began to grow with alarming rapidity.

'If you don't shut up, I'll ram your stinking teeth out the back of your revolting neck. I'll have you scraping dreck off a Golot looper's exhausts for the rest of your life.'

He was vaguely conscious that he had raised his voice a tone or so above the merely conversational. But, he assured himself, that was essential to penetrate the brutal and stupid mind of his colleague.

Bogie turned round at the raised voice and put his fingers to his lips with a saintly smile. 'Quite right, dear boy. Quite right.'

The fire had been extinguished, and it was hard to see the direction they'd been taking.

The blackness was so deep that Simon somehow found himself disconnected from Ensign Bogart. The idea that Bogart had gone and got himself lost was profoundly amusing, and he began to giggle. He laughed so much that he developed a pain in the back of his neck, and he had to force himself to stop. He wiped his eyes and looked round.

Overhead, the arch in the sky still glowed, but its light was fainter. The sickness returned, and he was alarmingly aware of what might happen if he were sick. The noise would waken up the enemy. But there was something far worse than that.

Simon sat down and pondered on the mechanism that caused and controlled vomiting. It was an automatic reaction that stopped one inhaling one's own puke and choking to death on it. But, he remembered in basics, if the mind wasn't in control, then that automatic mechanism might malfunction.

'But I'm in control. Yes. I am. I'm in control.' For a moment he wondered how that would sound if he sang it.

'Not a good idea. No good. Well in control.'

But the seeds of doubt had been planted by now. Maybe he wasn't in control. Somewhere in the darkness around him he thought he could hear a woman's voice, chanting a mantra.

'A mantra-chanter. Canter with a planter, to listen to the banter of a mantra-chanter.'

He giggled.

His mind wasn't in control ! !

That meant someone had drugged them in some way. Maybe the khetam had clawed him. Everyone knew that the khetam was a most unpleasant beast and that contact with it was something to be regretted.

Or were they doped? How? Why?

He was going to die. A tear of maudlin self-pity trickled down his cheek, furrowing a damp path through the dried dust. For a moment he wondered that there was still enough moisture in his tear-ducts to weep.

But he was going to die. He was going to be sick, and then his automatic muscles would become non-involuntary. The vomit would rise into his throat and then he would not be able to avoid inhaling it into his lungs. That would be it. He would die.

'I'm too young to die !' he screamed.

'Only the good die young,' he replied.

'True. Very true.' He found that thought of some consolation, and was grateful to himself for thinking of it.

Morning had broken. He bathed in the luxurious light for a while before he realised that it came from a torch of some kind held in the hand of

of a beautiful woman   each day she came to him and her   standing there clothed only in her fabled raiment . . . She always   an untouched maiden who had come from the hills to give him her help.

'Is that all?'

His voice sounded loud, ringing in his ears.

She'd vanished. No, there she was again. In front of him.

'Greetings from the Federation.' That was what they were told to say when meeting strange people for the first time. Not that she was strange.

A cloak of midnight that swirled   hair as black as the underside of the   flesh soft and firm   at the same   breast that pouted at him through the evening dullness of her gown   cones tipped with fire.

'I said . . . who are you?'

The girl looked at him gravely. Apart from the cloak, there seemed no other clothing. No. A small pouch at her waist, and thigh-length boots of dark skin.

Her face was impenetrable, hidden in the hood. Eyes glinting pale fire.

The eyes seeming to talk to him. To whisper to him of unknowable pleasure. Offering him the moist warm crevices of her body to fondle and twine in. Nibbling at the back of his mind with hints of half-heard corruption and sensuality.

All he could do was walk towards her. He had the colt in his hand. He didn't know why.

She pointed at it, a toss of the hood betraying a sudden doubt. Simon smiled at her, reassuringly. Feeling the smile threaten to slide from his face to lie leering in the red desert sand.

'Don't worry. It's broken.'

To prove it to her, he flung the weapon on the rocks, hearing the dull clang as it landed. The hint of concern vanished, and he caught the flash of white teeth in the cowled face.

Hand touching him gently where his maleness thrust towards her. Caressing and rousing him to a pitch he would never have believed possible. She held him, slowly turning his face up to meet hers. Her breasts brushed at his body.

The darkness of her hood eclipsed his face, smothering his eyes in its black velvet. Lips made the lightest contact and his hands went to her face.

And they felt thick, coarse skin. The skin of a woman aged beyond belief. He clawed at the face and strips of it fell apart in his hands. Layers of skin, yellow and mottled, flaked to the dirt. He screamed once and again. Livid eyes stared out from a charnel skull, blotched with the green of decay.

Still her hands gripped him, with an awful force that made him moan.

Then she struck him hard in the face, and twice more as he slumped to the warm sand. Struck him with a chrome statue of exquisite beauty.

There was no flash of truth or insight in his mind as he toppled hard into unconsciousness.

'I think that he will soon be with us once more. But his companion still sleeps.'

The voice seemed to come through a defective scrambler, washed across æons of garbled space. The words hung on the outside of his mind, but failed to penetrate or have any meaning. It might be a good idea to try and get his eyes open, but all the weight of inner space lay over them, holding them shut.

'Shall I waken him?'

The voice was that of a woman. A young woman. Soft and gentle.

With his eyes closed, Simon was still victim to the last dregs of terror. For a moment he saw himself running along a long corridor in an old, old house, with empty frames of paintings lining it. There were no doors, and the dusk lay heavy so that he could never see the end of it.

But over his shoulder he could hear quiet footfalls. Coming closer. However fast he ran, they were always faster. At last he could stand it no longer, and turned.

The hooded figure of a woman was sweeping nearer, the face hidden under the black cowl. The hands were folded in front, and the feet barely seemed to touch the floor.

He stood, stricken, facing her, as she drew closer to him. She stopped, nearly touching him, and he was aware of a faint smell from her gown. A heavy perfume that reminded him of tall arches and of chanting and candlelight.

She bent to kiss him and the cowl fell from her face.

Simon screamed.

Something struck him on the cheek, and twice more.

He opened his eyes and looked at the face of a young woman. Hooded and cloaked, her naked body visible as she leaned over him. He was lying down.

She smiled at him. 'You and your friend are very strong. Neither of you are from Zayin, are you?'

Faster now, control came back to Simon. They'd been drugged. Probably by a gas. That was why they'd behaved how they had. And why he'd seen what he thought he'd seen. But this girl wasn't a hallucination. And she was the woman whom he'd seen in the crater. Throbbing at his temple and the side of his face told him that he *had* been hit.

'You hit me?' It was really more of a statement than a question.

A smile on the face of the woman. 'Yes. I saw that you still held some control over yourself. It was the only way to find out who you were and what you wanted.'

His head almost clear, Simon sat up. His colt had been removed, and he had the feeling that his clothes had been taken from him and replaced while he was unconscious.

'Where's my colleague?'

'Right here, Simon.' Bogie walked into the chamber where he was, followed – or guarded? – by two men. His belt also lacked the parax-gun.

'Hello, Bogie. How're you feeling?'

'Like a tail section fell on my head. Apart from that, I'm ready for anything.'

While he spoke, Bogie's fingers had been plucking aimlessly at the side of his torn trousers. Simon had always done well on coding and signalling. The fingers told him to play it quiet and not give anything away.

Simon was surprised. Apart from the bruises, they seemed friendly enough. But in the short time he'd known Ensign Eugene Bogart he'd seen enough to know that Bogie didn't waste words or actions. If he said play it quiet, then that's what Simon would do.

The girl straightened up and Simon saw that she was very tall. The boots she wore to protect against the needle-sharp rocks made her taller, but she topped even him by several centimetres. Like the men, she went naked, but for a belt and pouch. And the boots. At night – he somehow felt it was still night – they wore cloaks.

Unsteadily, Simon stood up and clasped hands with Bogie. He gave a wry grin at his own weakness, then looked round the room. It was high and arched, hewn from the living rock, with the walls heavily painted and ornamented with intricate designs of great beauty.

He looked to the woman. 'This is Xoachtl, and you are what they call the arties?'

'Yes. And you are both members of the Federation's much-vaunted and powerful security service. We would know why you are here. What do you want with us?'

Conscious of Bogie's eyes digging into his back, Simon wondered what the hell he could answer to that. Tell the truth? Make up some credible story for their being out in the middle of the backlands?

'Wait, Daen. There can be no harm in waiting. Visitors here are rarer than the lake filling with stars. It cannot have been pleasant for them to undergo our . . . warning systems. Take them to a vacant dwelling and we will all talk to them later. Give them drink and food.'

Simon smiled thankfully at the speaker. An older man, his cloak thick and trimmed with fragile golden embroidery. Hair whitened against his bronzed skin. As he smiled, he was suddenly aware that it didn't hurt him. The swelling and dryness had gone, and his mouth felt normal.

The woman, Daen, watched him touching his face and guessed what he was thinking. 'While you were not with us, you were given drink through your skin, and your hurts were tended.'

He bowed his thanks.

The older man spoke. 'You will now go to your rest. Then we will learn from you why you are here, so far from what some men call the benefits of the cities. And why you had no water.'

Simon chose not to make any reply. Bogart spoke: 'Thanks to all of you for your help.' By a subtle inflection of voice he made it clear that had it not been for their hallucinogenic attack, they might have needed less help. 'Thanks mainly for the water.'

'All who pass our gates are under our protection and are given water.'

Before they went away, Daen had the last word. 'The main entrance to Xoachtl is called the Water Gate for that reason. You were in need, so we helped you.'

As they were escorted out, Bogart whispered to Simon: 'I'm glad to hear about their Water Gate.'

Simon whispered back: 'Yes. They had us taped all right.'

All of Simon's latent suspicions came to the surface the moment they were left on their own. He collapsed on the bed, feeling the effects of the drug more than the older, harder Bogie.

He jumped in alarm when Bogie instantly sat next to him on the bed, and put his arms round his shoulders. Their faces were so close to each other that he could feel the prickling of the stubble on Bogie's chin.

'What . . .?'

A horny hand over his mouth shut him up. Bogie pressed his lips as close as possible to his ear and spat out one word: 'Hum.'

'Mmmerrghmm,' he tried to speak, but the grip over his face didn't relax.

'Just hum!'

Deciding that Bogie was still under the influence of the

drug, Simon reckoned that he'd better humour him, and started an extremely muffled hum. The noise vibrated inside his head, but he could still hear Bogie's voice.

'May be sniffers. This stops them hearing. Don't you gravs learn anything? Any time we want to talk, use this way. Right?'

Simon nodded.

'I'm going to give this place a turning-over. I don't reckon they'll have sniffers in. Don't seem the sort. Still can't be too careful.'

Lying back on the bare bed, with its ornamental coverlet, Simon watched in silent admiration while his partner went round the dwelling. 'Partner.' Simon decided he liked the sound of the word.

It was an odd place where they'd been left by the arties. The walls seemed organic, slightly rough to the touch. There were no windows and only the one door. Walls curved in on themselves at odd angles, and there was an unusual feeling of impermanency about it.

Although it had been full dark when they were taken to it, Simon had been aware enough to see that the house was stuck in some mysterious way to the walls of the high cliffs. The cliffs that had been mined to make Xoachtl.

Finally, Bogie came back and sat on the other side of the bed. 'Clean. Far as I can tell. It's clean. Not a bug or a sniffer anywhere. Now, here we are. What next?'

Simon couldn't conceal his amazement. 'You're asking me what next?'

'Yes. Of course. I'm no tactician, Simon, my boy. I'm a sort of blunt instrument. Point me in the direction you want me to take, and I'll shoot my way through an army. But, ask me about planning and logistics, and my brain turns into a bowl of curdled vit-soup. No, it's all down to you, Simon. Look, if it helps, think aloud.'

Taking a deep breath, Simon began. 'Right. We know what got us here. This is Xoachtl. It does exist. And it looks like it is the headquarters of the arties. So, we reckon that Corman might be in some sort of plot to get here and help the thinkers against them.'

He paused. Bogie looked across at him. 'What are you waiting for? A medal? That's how I see it. I want you to tell me what we do about it?'

They were interrupted by a shuddering of the room, like a muscular spasm. That was what Bogie said. Laughing nervously at the absurdity of it. It seemed much less funny when it was repeated more strongly a couple of seconds later.

Outside they heard shouting and feet running. One of the arties, his cloak tangled up round his knees, climbed in, sweat trickling off his high cheeks. 'Quickly. The sirque is about to move to a new site. I'll take you to another one.'

Outside, they blinked in the bright light of many torches, waving in the cool wind that heralded the approach of dawn. Urged on by the crowd, they clambered down the spider-thin ladders until they felt rock beneath their feet.

The girl, Daen, was there, and she took Simon's arm and pointed up. 'See. We regret that you are disturbed by this, but the movements of our sirques are difficult to predict. Watch.'

To their amazement, the whole round house above them was shaking, like some creature in the throes of death. But this wasn't death. It was merely a change of habitat.

As Daen explained, the sirque was indeed a living creature. It had an ideal symbiotic relationship with the humans. But the drawback was that it was still ambulatory. When it wished, it would simply roll its way from one part of the rugged cliff face to another. The shaking they had experienced was the only warning. As it rolled, the walls constricted and pulsed, causing anybody left inside the risk of severe and possibly fatal injuries.

Once it had found another locale it fancied, it would

tether itself and again become a safe and secure dwelling.

'How often does it do that?'

'Not frequently. Sometimes many months pass.'

There was a thin cracking from above them, and shards of splintered rock pattered about their heads, making them all duck away. The sphere, brightly painted and decorated on the outside by the arties, was rolling slowly away from were it had been, moving ponderously up and to the left.

'Come. It will settle where it wishes. You will be taken to another sirque. Tomorrow we will talk.'

And she left them.

Once they were alone again, they picked up the tangled threads of their last conversation.

'Come on then, Simon. Tell us what to do.'

The boy's forehead crinkled with the effort of thought. Although he'd taken part in plenty of simulated exercises, he was chillingly aware that all the exercises in the universe were little use when the real thing came along. If their suspicions were correct, then Corman could be there to dabble in a fragile political situation that could topple into frenzied chaos.

He coughed to clear his throat, suddenly dry again. 'Well. Suppose we tell them. The arties. That we think Corman is in league with the thinkers to try and attack this place and take away their influence. Maybe even destroy them.'

'I reckon we have to tell them. But that'll be for tomorrow. Now it's sleep time.'

'As long as this damned thing doesn't go rolling off again with us in it.'

'Still. I enjoy having a ball every now and again.'

'Good night, Bogie.'

'Good night, Simon.'

There was silence for a couple of minutes. Then Bogie whispered across the space between them : 'Hey, Simon.'

'What?'

66

'You're all right.'

Simon Rack went to sleep still smiling with pleasure.

Both men slept well, and were only woken by the first golden rays of the sun crawling across their bodies. Like all days on Zayin, it was going to be fine and hot.

The older man, Hualpa, came with a handful of other arties to take them to the meeting. The men were naked, but for the boots and loincloths, with a pouch at their waist. The cloaks had been abandoned after the chill of the night.

They were greeted courteously but distantly, and offered food. It was drink that their stomachs craved more than anything, and they asked for both liquids and solids.

'I will return to you after you have broken your fasts, and we will talk. We wish to know why you are here. Why your Federation has chosen to send you at this time above all. But eat and drink. Talk comes later.'

'If at all,' muttered Bogie after the arties had all gone.

There were trays of food. Strips of some kind of dried meat, softened in creamy sauces, with artificial vegetables. Unbearably sweet puddings, heavy and frozen somewhere deep within Xoachtl. Best of all were the drinks. Pale green, flecked with silver shreds of ice, served in wonderful goblets of gleaming chrome and crystal.

While they ate and drank, they agreed the final points of their story.

'We gloss over the killings. Tell them about Corman and the thinker and leave the rest to them. Right?'

Bogart nodded. 'Right. Thank God I feel a bit better than last night. That hally they pumped at us was a bastard. A real bastard.'

They drained their drinks and went outside, blinking at the yellow glare. Their sirque rested quiescently against the baked red rock, its brightly-painted sides contrasting oddly with the harshness of the mountain.

They climbed down the wavering ladders into the natural arena at the base of the cliff. Eons ago water would have cascaded from high above, carving out the bowl – a full hundred metres across. But that was centuries in the past. No water had touched that barren waste for many years. Heat expanded it and the cold shrank and split it.

The colours blended from the palest of yellows to deep oranges and browns. Ore deposits splashed darker patches on the higher slopes. They paused together to gaze across the backlands towards the faintest smudge of smoke on the furthest horizon. That was the city of Fort Peine. Although it was still early, heat haze made it difficult to see any distance with any clarity.

'Hurry. The council are waiting to hear from you.'

There was a nudge in the back for Simon to remind him that their position was nearer prisoner than guest. The arties that shepherded them inside the corridors of the cliffs of Xoachtl were armed with blasters tucked into their heavily ornamented belts. Although there was no obvious threat, they were left in no doubt as to their true status.

The dank caverns were lit by flickering tubes, glowing with an eerie, red-tinged flame. The walls were everywhere covered in bright paintings, swirling designs of unimagined colours, mingling and melting into the blackness between the lights. Their feet echoed ahead of them, and they were handed over to another party of guards.

'These paintings must be worth a premier's ransom,' muttered Simon, peering upwards at some of the higher pictures that sprawled clear up to the vaulted roofs of the corridor.

'They reckon they keep the finest specimens hidden away somewhere in the middle of this damned warren.'

A jab in the back from a fist shut them up. A huge door of some dull metal, chased with ornate floral engravings, barred their way. A voice crackled out of a concealed speaker and the leader of their party whispered the password back. With a soft hiss the right-hand door swung open and they marched through it.

They found themselves in a semi-circular arena, with rows of seats towering up towards the ceiling. But the room was so big that the dim lights didn't penetrate that far. There were certainly seats there for at least ten thousand people.

They were occupied by less than five hundred.

A row of chairs at the front was filled by what were obviously the senior members of the tribe. The man who had spoken up for them, Hualpa, was near the centre. Daen, one of the youngest there, was at the extreme end of the row. She gazed at them with an incurious blankness.

The biggest seat – almost a throne – stood at the middle, its back and sides encrusted with glowing stones. It was occupied by a frail man, whose paper-white hair rolled over his shoulders. With an obvious effort he struggled to his feet and smiled.

'Welcome to Xoachtl, the home of the last and only true artists' colony on Zayin. The cities of the south are dying and there is little beauty left to us. My name is Aenghs, and I am the last father of Xoachtl.'

Simon bowed to the old man. 'I think you know who we are. I am a midman in the Inter-Galactic Security Service. My name is Simon Kennedy Rack. This man is my friend and . . . partner. Ensign Eugene Bogart. We are glad to be here and we thank you for the warmth of your welcome. Though . . .' he rubbed the bruises on his face ruefully, 'there were elements of the welcome that might, perhaps, have been omitted.'

There was a ripple of laughter. Daen's face still remained unmoved. Aenghs smiled.

'Aye. Our women have always been ready for action. More ready, I think, than many of the men. But we would know why you are here. You know that few outlanders have ever penetrated this place.'

'And lived.'

The voice was bitter. Hoarse with emotion. It came from a young man sitting in the front row, three seats along from Daen. He half-rose, as though intending to say more, then thought better of it and sat down again.

'As you see, Simon and Eugene, there are those among the young who would have us revert to our old ways.' He turned to the man and addressed him directly. 'Recall, Niokl, that this has been talked over for many debates, and it was the will of the majority. Was it not?'

Eyes downcast, Niokl nodded his head.

'Niokl is unhappy that the old ways have changed. There was a time, and that time was very recent, that any man who came upon Xoachtl would never tell of it. The gas that stunned you was weaker than that we used before. If it had been at full strength, then you would have become permanently mad, or you would have died.'

'May I ask, Aenghs, why you have changed your ways?'

Again it was the young man, Niokl, who shouted out: 'No! Let us hear their story first. They merely try to buy themselves time.'

The old man's voice cracked out like a neural whip. 'Be silent. I will take action against you if you dare to interrupt the workings of the council one more time. If I choose to answer the question, then I will do so. Then we will hear their story. Is that clear?'

Face pale with anger, Niokl sat down again.

Aenghs turned to Simon and Bogart. 'You must know of our history. Of our conflict with the scientists. The men you call the thinkers. This world is near to the critical level and there are those who say it cannot survive. We artists have always been the rulers of morals. But we have kept ourselves distant. Relying only on the infrequent sales of our works to survive. Now our position has become desperate. There is no longer sufficient call on Zayin for what we produce. So we have decided to open our inner chambers and sell off a small number of our finest sculptures and paintings to outworlders.'

There was a mutter from around the cavern, but Aenghs ignored it and pressed on. 'But only a very few. Xoachtl contains not only the finest collection anywhere in any galaxy of artwork of all kinds. It also keeps the secret of how we have been able . . .' In his excitement at what he was saying the old man had gone further than he intended.

It was Daen who interrupted him : 'Father! No more! You must not profane our greatest secret.'

He stopped and rubbed his head, looking momentarily confused. 'I . . . I . . . regret that my enthusiasm . . . you were right to reproach me.' With an effort he pulled himself together and carried on 'So that is why you are here alive. If the thinkers were to gain access here, we would be defeated.'

Trying to concentrate on what was being said, Simon found his thoughts wandering. He had seen the way the arties lived. A life little better than menial labourers on a dozen frontier worlds. Yet they still saw themselves as leaders of the planet. The dying, wasted, barren, useless, charred splinter of carbon called Zayin.

He knew well enough how false were their ideas of rebirth. There was just enough to Zayin to persuade the Federation to help it with grants. But that aid was constantly being cut back and back. One day Zayin would cease to have even the bare importance it now had.

And it would end.

But Aenghs was going on. Something about help.

'So. Because we felt we could trust nobody on this world to aid us in our dealings, we have contacted an outworlder to help. I expect him shortly. He will advise us on how to best dispose of some of our work at best profit. Then we will once again show the scientists who runs Zayin.'

There was scattered applause, though Simon noticed that it came mainly from the older men and women. After a pause the others joined in, including Daen. Niokl sat still, his eyes fixed on the two GalSec officers.

His face transformed by the cheering, Aenghs smiled at the two strangers. 'Now you know of our plans. I think that the time has come for you to tell us what your plans are. Why are you here?'

Simon turned to glance at Bogie, who grinned at him encouragingly and motioned for him to launch into the story they'd agreed.

'Gentlemen and ladies. I . . .' He stopped and coughed, stricken with the sudden feeling that his voice was going to betray him and crack into a falsetto squeak.

'My colleague and I are here as a result of many odd adventures. It began when we were . . .'

He stopped when he saw that he had lost part of his audience. Heads had turned and a buzz of whispering sidled round the huge chamber. A young artie had come hurrying in, going straight to Aenghs, bending low and muttering urgently in his ear. The old man had looked up and peered into the shadows behind Simon and Bogart.

Realising that Simon had checked his speech, Aenghs waved a vague hand at him. 'Quite, quite. There is a new development here. Our friend has come to assist us. Perhaps he too will be interested in hearing your tale.' He raised his voice and called to the guards on the main doors : 'Have him brought in to us !'

There was the sound of feet pattering on the stone floor and Simon and Bogart both swung round to watch the newcomer. He was a tall, willowy youth, his blond hair trimmed neatly to his shoulders. He wore a patterned tunic and sandals with gold stacked heels. Even in the dim light they could see he wore facial make-up.

Bogie sniffed. 'I can smell his damned scent from here. The arties have got themselves a fine hesher. Remind me to keep my back to the wall when he passes by.'

'Quiet ! He'll hear you.'

But the young man had paused several paces from them, looking up to the council in their double rows. Waving his arm in a delicate gesture, he bowed low, his hair almost sweeping the floor.

'I bring you greetings from my master. Come here to aid the men and women of Xoachtl in their struggle against the forces of oppression. My master is without and will soon be within.'

'Without what?' muttered Bogie.

Aenghs smiled. 'You and your master are welcome here. Ask him to come in and join us. We are about to hear a story that may intrigue him. For he is not the only outworlder within these cliffs.'

The young boy peered at Simon and Bogie, as though seeing them for the first time. He sniffed. Very audibly. 'My master will not be pleased at this.'

Simon felt he had stood silent long enough. 'Why not tell your master and then let him come and tell us if he finds our presence here so offensive.'

There was a snort from the lake of blackness at the rear of the chamber, followed by laughter. Heavy footfalls, slow and ponderous, coming closer.

A deep and throaty voice : 'Well, well. My young friend. A wise man once said that once is happenstance and twice is coincidence. The third time it is the action of an enemy.'

Aenghs rose, beaming. 'You must be . . .?'

'Harley Corman, sir. At your service.'

FIVE

The Bells of the Crown

A name circled in Simon's mind, toppling and whirling like an animated vid. The letters wandered across the blank screen inside his skull, swirling and rearranging into patterns that became words.

Harley Corman. A fat, unctuous man. Smiling only with his mouth, and rarely with his eyes.

The name became another. Casper Gutman.

Why?

He concentrated hard, trying to work out why. Suddenly a bird flew past him. Wings flapping so slowly that it seemed it must plummet to earth, or crash into the bitter lake where Simon would soon die.

A falcon.

He was pleased with himself for recognising it.

The sun grazed his eyes, and he half-closed them, squinting up at the cliff face that towered above him. Wondering for a passing moment whether Bogie had got Ahmed.

Pleased that he could care about that at such a time.

'Well done, Rack.' As he giggled, his voice sounded heavy and blurred. Deep and slow.

There couldn't be much time left. He seemed to have been falling for minutes.

As an experiment, he tried closing his eyes again, conscious of slight nausea at the weaving motion.

It was dark.

Dark.

Dark.

The cavern seemed smaller and darker at the appearance of Harley Corman.

Bogart, unflappable as he usually was, gasped at the sight of Corman. The man they had been about to reveal to the assembled arties as a villain. As a man whom they suspected of plotting the downfall of the colony at Xoachtl.

Simon's mind raced. Corman had moved within a few paces of him, the little eyes among the rolls of fat as keen as crystal lasers.

'Well, my young sir. Do I understand that you are about to tell these good folk why you and your jolly friend are so far from your homes? Pray do not let me detain you in any way. You see,' he addressed the interested Aenghs, 'I have made the acquaintanceship of these young men before. In Fort Peine a day or so ago. At an eating-house. I trust they will remember that. We discussed two pieces of very dead meat that the house served.'

For a moment Simon had the odd impression that he had been clubbed in the centre of his brain. His head seemed to be filled with soft wadding. Try as he might, no single constructive thought was able to find a way out.

Corman continued, pitching his voice lower, so that the menace would only carry to the two officers. 'Dead meat. Nasty sight, young sirs, if you take my meaning. It would grieve me exceedingly to see two more such pieces of meat.'

Had he waved a neural spray at them, his threat couldn't have been more obvious.

Aenghs and the other arties had been straining their ears, trying to overhear what had passed between the two men. Corman pasted his smile more firmly in place and turned back to face the council. 'A few thoughts for my brave young comrades here. Forgive me.'

The willowy youth coughed meaningfully. Corman shrugged his vast shoulders and waved at the young man. 'Of course. My dear Aenghs, members of the praesidium of the artists' colony of Xoachtl. Permit me to introduce my assistant. His name is Joel Wilburson. He accompanies me everywhere.'

The leader of the arties made a short speech of welcome, inviting their new guests to come and sit by him on the raised platform. Simon noticed how Corman wheezed and panted at the effort of climbing even the short flight of stairs. He really was grossly fat. Once they were all settled, eyes turned again to Simon and Bogart.

'I'm sorry that you were interrupted, Midman Rack. You may now go on with your story.'

Everyone, including Corman, leaned forward to catch the words. All, that is, except the handsome young Joel, who picked his nose avidly, examining what he found there carefully before transferring it to his cupid's bow of a mouth.

Simon could almost feel the surface of his brain buzzing with electrical energy as he frantically tried to think of some story he could tell. The appearance of Corman, already in a position of trust, had shot everything to hell and back.

'We have come here because we were falsely accused of two killings in the back streets of Fort Peine. The hunt was up for us and we felt that there was only one place on this planet where we might find safety and justice. Here in Xoachtl.'

There was a brief silence. He heard the sharp whistle of Bogie's indrawn breath behind him. Then chatter broke out all around the chamber. Aenghs stood shakily up and waved his hands, helplessly trying to quiet his people.

Simon snatched the chance to have a quick word with Bogie at his side : 'If you can think of a better story – it's too sodding late to use it.'

'It is,' said Bogart grimly. Adding : 'But I couldn't.'

'Quiet! Quiet!! Thank you. Quiet.' At last there was a sort of silence. Simon saw Corman watching the happenings like a contented khetam, a grin dribbling over his gigantic jowls. The boy, Joel, sat close to him, and Corman leaned

76

across and whispered to him. His lips brushed softly against the lad's cheeks.

'So. We thought you had come as either ambassadors or spies. You come simply as fugitives from justice.'

Niokl rose to his feet, his clenched fist beating at the table in front of him. 'No! I am sure they are spies. Why do we not kill them? Or return them to their damned Federation?'

The girl, Daen, also stood up. 'We have ruled that we will not kill. And their ship has been gone for a day. We cannot return them.'

'Daen. You have the sight. Are they spies?'

She turned her face to the old man, the light gleaming on her oiled body, the breasts proudly jutting out. 'I cannot always see, Aenghs. Perhaps if I had some time with them, I could find the truth.'

On an impulse, Simon spoke. 'We'll submit to any test of our honesty. We are not killers. We are not spies. We do not wish any harm to come to Xoachtl or to the arties ... artists.'

Corman leaned across and tugged at the chief's arm. The old man sat down and listened. Then shook his head violently. Stood up again.

'We have listened to what you say. I am for returning you to the backlands for the desert there to try you. But I will put it to the vote. Who wishes these men to be imprisoned by us and tested for truth?'

They looked round quickly, seeing about half the hands go up.

'And who wishes them taken out?'

Perhaps a few hands more went up.

'Very well. For sending to the backlands there is needed a clear majority. I do not think there was one. Take them away.'

As they were led off by the armed arties, Simon's last glance at the fat man showed him beaming benevolently at them. While his right hand was busy somewhere in the lap of his boy.

Bogart also saw that and spat contemptuously on the sandy floor. 'I bet that flaming hesher is so fond of Corman he'd bend over backwards for him.'

Their laughter seemed to drive back the looming shadows for a moment.

The sirque they were taken to was fixed to the rocky wall at a lower level and was a little away from the rest of the encampment. The ornamentation was less bright – mainly black and silver circles, swirling around, mingling and separating.

With two guards on the door, it made an effective prison. After Aenghs called to see them the guards were removed, but they were left on their honour not to attempt to get out. The old man was obviously upset by the turn that things had taken, but he wasn't prepared to risk the safety of Xoachtl on a whim.

'Although I had wished you removed, the will of my people was not for it. Violence is not in our creed, but we are ruthless with those who lie and threaten our existence. Had I been given my way, you would have been armed and given enough water for you to have a chance to reach one of the cities. Now if you are found to be lying, then your lot will be harder. You will be banished to the backlands with neither food nor drink nor weapons.'

His words had hooked into their minds, and they'd argued bitterly about what they should do. Bogie was for breaking out and trying to steal enough supplies to get away.

'No. Listen to me, Bogie. They've got these gases and God knows what else. Two. We've given our words. Three. We know we're telling the truth. If we can convince this girl, then we've got a chance of beating Corman. We *have* to stay here.'

Irritably Bogart kicked a chair into the corner, where it banged hard against the wall of the sirque. To their horror, the whole wall flicked inwards at them, and the structure seemed to groan. After that they were more careful.

Time passed. So slowly.

At last – from the heat inside the sirque they guessed it must be near the middle of the day – they heard boot-heels clicking across the rock. A figure darkened the doorway and in came Daen. As before she was naked above the waist. Her leather pouch was delicately ornamented with golden filigree and her boots were patterned and studded. She was very tall.

Simon felt his pulse rate increase at the sight of her bare breasts. But the sheathed dagger at her hip cooled his passion a little.

Stooping slightly, she smiled grimly at them. 'Well. I can only listen to one of you. Which is it to be?'

Bogart grinned crookedly up at her. 'I think you're too high above me to hear anything I might say. Better take young Simon here.'

She didn't answer. Merely turned and left the room, beckoning Simon after her. There was time for a quick hand-clasp and then Simon followed.

Bogie hissed a warning after him, but it's doubtful if he heard it. 'Make sure you tie your ankles to the bedpost. Otherwise she'll swallow you whole.'

He was alone. As he sat down, he muttered : 'Or, maybe it should be hole.'

Daen led him to a small sirque, high up on the cliffs, some distance from the nearest house. It was painted in designs that matched her belt.

'Did you do that yourself?' asked Simon, pointing to the flowing silver and gold designs.

'Yes.'

She ducked inside, and Simon scrambled in off the ladders after her. It was dark, with only the reflected light of the golden sun sliding in to lie across the floor like a dappled carpet. The room contained a bed, a table, and a small chair.

She pointed to the chair, and sprawled across the bed. It had been a hard climb, but the slow rise and fall of her breasts showed how fit she was.

'Very well, Simon Rack. Look at me, hold my hands in yours, and tell me your story again.'

He pulled the chair closer and held her hands, marvelling how cool they were. Her eyes were brown, flecked with gold, and he stared fixedly into them.

Just as he was about to speak, he noticed something. 'Your eyes.'

'What about them?'

'The pupils are very distended. You've taken some kind of drug.'

Pieces of jigsaw slotted into place, and he could see more of the picture. 'Drugs. That's how you'll tell whether I'm lying or not. The stories are true. You arties do have some secret drug that gives you power over minds.' But he was suddenly puzzled. 'Why don't you use it to get power? If that's what you want.'

The girl sat back, tugging her hands free. Anger flashed in her eyes and her hand went, almost unconsciously, to her knife. 'So! It is true what Corman told us. You are a spy, here to discover our weaknesses. Rob us of our precious . . .'

She stopped abruptly, realising she had been on the further edge of betrayal.

Tension hung between them like a curtain of beaded glass. Simon's mind raced to try and come up with an answer to the dangerous situation. He could tell that she was on the verge of leaving. Telling what she suspected. Condemning them to their deaths.

He saw her muscles tense. 'Wait! Listen to me, Daen. For the sake of your people. Before you hear me tell my story, let me tell you one thing. You can see if I'm lying?'

Warily, she nodded. 'Yes. I can tell when there is truth and when there are lies. What is this one thing you would tell me?'

Simon could hardly control the pounding in his chest. He stretched out his hands and again clasped hers. His eyes moved unwillingly from her breasts to stare again into the deeps of her eyes. She leaned a little forward, lines of concentration on her face.

'Are you ready, Daen?'

'Yes. But be warned. I have no tricks. I *will* be able to see. If you lie, then you and your friend are as good as dead.'

'Right. I will tell you one thing only. It is this. Neither my friend nor I wish anything but good to Xoachtl and the people in it. We have come here to help.'

For an uncanny moment he seemed to feel ghostly fingers, probing and caressing inside his head. Then she smiled at him. 'I am glad of that. You speak the truth. But why did Corman say what he did?'

'Did you test him?'

She shook her head. 'No. It never occurred to any of us that he might be other than honest. Perhaps we should have done. But your story before the council – was it not true?'

Quickly, still holding her hands, Simon told Daen the whole story. The only thing he omitted was the reason for his presence at the bordello.

She heard him out in silence, her eyes never leaving his. When he'd finished, she let go of his hands and lay back across the bed.

Daen's face was troubled. 'You really think the scientists would do this? Hire a man to steal our finest works? It doesn't seem possible.'

There was another possibility that had occurred to Simon, and he wondered whether to tell the girl or keep it to himself.

His dilemma was resolved for him. Daen sat up and

stared hard at him again. 'A new thought has come to you. Tell me what it is.'

'All right. I'm not all that bright, but I'm not a fool. You can do this . . . this mind-reading bit . . . by using some drug or other. Don't you?'

There was a long pause. Daen licked her lips nervously, fingers playing with the hilt of her knife.

'You don't have to answer, Daen. Silence tells me all I want to know. I've heard that much of your best art is also done under the influence of some precious drug. Suppose someone got their hands on that. Think what power it might give an unscrupulous person.'

'Someone like Corman?'

'Someone like Corman.'

To his amazement, Daen slumped back on the bed and began to weep, her shoulders shaking as she cried. A sobbing woman was something that Simon had never experienced. Well, not since he'd left the castle. He sat there blushing like an idiot, wondering what he could do. Tentatively, he reached out and patted her gingerly on the shoulder. Much as one would a frightened horse.

She grabbed it and squeezed it, making him wince with pain. Daen really didn't know her own strength. In between sobs, she gasped out what he'd already guessed. There *was* a drug, called atica. It was a sort of fungus that they had been unable to develop artificially. Although generations of their best minds had tried. The only place it grew was deep in the black chambers beneath Xoachtl, a strange by-product of chemical action and biological mutation.

'The thing is, Simon, there is very little of atica left. It grows terribly slowly. That's why I'm the only one in the whole of Xoachtl who's allowed to use it for probing. Years ago, everyone had as much as they wanted of it, so that they could expand their minds and produce their best work. The trouble was, everyone used it and supplies dropped almost to nothing.'

'Could I see it? And see your treasures?'

'No. No, I'm sorry, Simon. That's out of the question for you. Do you think that Corman is after all these things? After our paintings and sculptures? After atica? *And* helping the thinkers to destroy us?'

Simon nodded. 'I fear so, Daen. From what I know of Harley Corman, his ambitions are as big as his body.'

To his relief, some of the tension slipped away from her face, and she laughed. 'He *is* fat. Somehow, you think that fat men like him must either be idle or jolly and friendly. You don't think of wicked fat men.' Still laughing, she pulled him down beside her on the bed. 'You're very young, Simon Rack. How old are you?'

'Twenty,' he said hastily, forgetting her power.

Daen smacked his wrist. 'No. It doesn't matter to me that you're still a young boy. I'm nearly eight years older than you, but it doesn't matter to me. Does it matter to you?'

Before he could answer, she tugged his head down, lifting her face to meet him. Her lips, warm and soft, pressed against his, while her fingers tangled in his hair. He returned her kiss, feeling clumsy against her experience. Daen's tongue pushed at his lips, insistently probing until he allowed it entrance.

In turn, she sucked his tongue into her sweet-tasting mouth, tangling and licking. He gasped for breath, and pulled away.

She put her hand lightly on his shoulder. ' I want you to take me. Penetrate me, Simon. Now.'

There was a light curtain hanging above the doorway of the sirque, and he got up and lowered it over the entrance. Darkness swam into the round room – a rich, golden, glowing darkness – and he blinked across at Daen as she wriggled her way out of her belt.

'Pull my boots off for me, Simon.'

Somehow, it made him blush to see her so totally naked, though he had almost got used to watching her semi-nude as she, and the other women in Xoachtl, moved about. He grasped the smooth leather and tugged her boots off, throwing them in the corner with a dull thud.

For a moment he simply stood and looked down at her, lying on the bed, her legs partly spread, a gentle smile on her face. She was like a beautiful fish, trapped in the yellow light at the bottom of some bizarre aquarium.

'Come to me, Simon. Or are you simply going to stand and look?'

He made a move to join her on the bed, when she held up her hand. 'Aren't you going to take off that stuffy uniform, or is it one of your GalSec regulations that officers must keep their trousers on at all times?'

Her giggle had a wanton sensuality to it that he had never heard before. The sound that he had imagined as he had lain in his lonely bunk in the bowels of the *Venturer*. A sound that made it hard to struggle out of his trousers, as they got hooked up on a prominent obstruction.

At last he too was naked, and he hopped across to her like a skinned frog, embarrassed by his erection probing the air before him.

Daen put him at his ease, reaching out and fondling him with her cool strong fingers. 'Your sensor seems to know where it wants to go, Simon.'

He lay beside her, hands nervously feeling for her breasts, squeezing them, grinning as the nipples responded to his touch. She rolled on top of him, kissing him hard, using her fingers to keep him aroused.

'Touch me here. No, here.'

Wondering, he felt his fingers enter her warm moistness, making her moan and writhe. At last she flopped back and guided him into her.

The next few minutes passed in a rich haze. Everything that Simon had read and heard and hoped about the act of love came true for him on that dying world.

When it was over, he lay still, heart pounding as though

he'd just run a foot race over a mountain range. Daen smiled up at him. Raised her hand and brushed the red mark on his shoulder where she'd bitten him at the moment of orgasm.

'That was very good, Simon Rack. Was it good for you?'

A quick answer jumped to his lips, and he choked it back. There had been the temptation to be worldly about it. To accept it as an everyday occurrence.

But he didn't.

He eased himself off her and lay back, gazing at the dome-shaped ceiling. Gently Simon's hand touched Daen on the cheek. 'It was my first time.'

She raised herself on to an elbow and looked gravely into his eyes. 'I am glad that it was with me.'

Outside there was the faint rattling noise of someone moving on a ladder. With a rueful grin at Simon, Daen jumped up to go over to the doorway.

'Duty calls us, my love. I suppose we must go to Aenghs and the council to tell them what you have told me. Afterwards . . . maybe we'll come back here.'

The curtain rustled and she went outside on to the narrow platform in front of the door.

As Simon sat up and began to pull his trousers on, he heard a gasp from beyond the curtain. He stood up, worried by the noise, then relaxed as Daen came back in.

'Simon . . .'

The voice was so quiet that he hardly heard it. The fastening on his trousers stubbornly resisted him, and he didn't look up.

'Simon . . .'

Louder, but with a harsh note of strain. Simon Rack looked up.

Her magnificent body naked, Daen swayed forwards at him. Blood splattered from a savage wound in her throat, cascading down across her breasts and over her stomach.

85

Clogging in her pubic hair, streaming on her thighs, to dribble down her legs to the floor.

As she moved, she left bloody footprints.

Bile rose in his chest as he saw what had been done to her. Unexpectedly, tears came to his eyes. Young and inexperienced though he was, he had done enough in the medic department, dealing especially with wounds, to know when a fatal blow had been struck.

He was able to catch her as she slumped forward, a warm spray of blood dashing into his face. Her eyes were open, staring up at him with a puzzled expression on her face. Carefully he laid Daen on the bed, watching helplessly as her lifeblood jetted out from the brutal rip in her throat.

Her fingers closed on his and her lips moved. He bent over, trying to catch her whispered words. 'Corman's . . . boy . . . outside . . . Knife in . . .'

The only sound was her rasping breath, getting weaker. Simon knew well that her assassin might still be there, and he ached to get out and slaughter him. Tear his body apart with his bare hands.

But the girl was dying. He would not have her die alone.

The grip on his hand relaxed and the breathing faded away to nothing. Simon glanced down and saw that the gouts of bright blood had slowed to a thin, irregular trickle. Daen's face and body were pale, even in the ochre glow through the curtain. Her eyes had closed and her expression was composed and still.

Laying the head of the corpse softly back, Simon reached out for where her belt lay. Where she had carelessly thrown it before they had made love. Sticking out from it was the hilt of her knife. A double-edged blade, ornamented and superbly engraved. The hilt was bound with thin strips of leather and the balance as it lay in the palm of his hand was perfect.

Wiping the sweat from his fingers, Simon braced himself for the charge at the doorway. A breath of wind puffed at the heavy curtain, making the pools of light dance and mingle on the floor, dappling the splodges of dark blood.

There had been creaking on the ladders, but it could have been someone else moving on the network of ropes. He stepped towards the door.

With a rush that ripped the curtain off its supports, two men came crashing into the sirque, grappling desperately with each other. Both men held knives, one of them streaked with blood.

One was dark-skinned, wearing only the belt of the arties. The other was slender, with a shock of tousled blond hair. The bright light breaking through the opened doorway glinted on the gold heels of his sandals. It was Joel Wilburson, and it was his knife that was stained with Daen's blood.

They rolled around, and Simon had to leap agilely aside to avoid them. The fight was so close and bitter that he couldn't yet see who the artie was.

For a moment they broke apart, and he saw and recognised the sullen face of the young man, Niokl, who had been opposed to them in the council meeting. In turn he recognised Simon and snarled bitterly. 'So! The two of you are allies. You will still not find it easy.'

The willowy youth caught a flash of a chance and made a despairing dive for the door. But Simon was quicker. His foot shot out, catching the murderer on the ankle.

His hands went out to save himself, but the fall was too sudden. Joel crashed on his stomach with a thump that sent the breath whooshing from his lungs. The dagger went spinning across the floor, ending up by Niokl's feet.

Joel struggled to his knees, teeth pulled back from his gums as he fought for air. Watched in bewilderment by the arty, Simon took one fluid step forward and lashed out with his bare foot. It caught Wilburson in the throat, and he fell back, writhing in agony. Blood trickled between his lips where he'd bitten through the end of his tongue.

Niokl ignored the moaning man and pushed past Simon to look down at Daen's body on the blood-soaked bed. When he turned away, his face was expressionless.

'Rack. I was coming to see if you and Daen had completed your questioning. I saw this,' pointing with his knife at the figure of Joel Wilburson, 'creeping up the ladder towards this sirque. I followed him. Saw Daen come out. Saw him slash at her with his blade. That's all.'

Quickly Simon and Niokl tied up the injured boy in strips cut from the bedding. Then they hoisted him to his feet and hobbled his feet, leaving just enough slack to enable him to get down the ladders. During the operation, Joel didn't speak, sobbing to himself and coughing up blood from his bruised throat.

Once it was done, Simon faced Niokl. 'I was telling the truth to Daen. Corman is a criminal who wishes to destroy your whole community and take your treasures.'

Dark eyes peered at him. 'This happening shows there may be truth in what you say. But how can I be sure of you?'

Simon gave him the one word : 'Atica.'

Niokl whistled and dropped his head. 'So. She told you that. Then she believed you. Come, we must go to the council and tell them of this. Aenghs is meeting with other elders at this moment. We can go to him.'

The gold light was waning away, with the Arch of Zayin hanging blackly overhead, as they made their perilous way down towards the ground. Joel moaned and cried with fear at the descent, unable to cling to the ladders with his hands bound. Halfway down it became obvious that he was in genuine danger of falling and Simon reluctantly slashed through the cords, leaving the hobble on his ankles.

At last Simon, who was leading, felt the rough grittiness of the rocks beneath his feet. In a matter of moments they were in the cool shade of the corridors.

The hesher was still crying as he was hustled along in the

semi-darkness. Niokl led the way through the twisting labyrinth, attracting curious glances from the occasional arty
that they passed.

'I can't wait to see that fat pig's face,' said Niokl, turning
a blank corner.

'Is there any particular porcine creature that you wish
to meet?' The voice was rich and deep, pitched low enough
for them to hear, but not loud enough for them to pin down
where it came from.

'Corman!' gasped Niokl. His hand went to his belt and
he pulled out the knife, backing towards Simon and their
prisoner.

'At your service. I lament to see that my young companion is being so ill-served by you. I fear that the council
will not be pleased, if you take my meaning.'

'Your young catamite has killed Daen! And we know all
about your plans.'

There was a soft chuckle from the blackness. 'Indeed.
Midman Rack, you really are a most infuriating young
fellow. I cannot tolerate your continued interference in my
unimportant scheme of things. I assume that dear Joel there
had his wrist slapped and promptly . . . what's the good old-
fashioned expression I want . . .? Yes. Spilled the food to
you. Tut, tut, Joel. Such a lack of gratitude saddens me.'

The arty and Simon had put the hesher behind them,
away from that cultured, mocking voice. Joel was weeping
loudly, falling to his knees.

'Harley. Dear darling; I didn't betray you. They knew.
Rack knew. I heard him tell the girl, so I shut her up. Like
you wanted me to.'

A sigh, as soft as a drop of poison in a goblet of rich wine.
'Goodbye, Joel.'

A crack like a whip and a bolt of power that ripped between Simon and Niokl, throwing the sobbing boy against
the rough-hewn wall. His ornate clothes flared and scorched.
In the ruddy light of the flames Simon saw that the missile

had hit Joel cleanly in the chest, blasting out a hole big enough for a man's fist. It had killed him instantly.

Blood hissed as it ran into the flames, gradually subduing them and finally extinguishing them. Simon had dropped instinctively to one knee, ready to break for cover. The part of the corridor where they had been stopped was ill-lit. But the part where the killer waited was in total darkness.

After the first moment of shock, Niokl acted. His feet grated on the sand as he dashed for the place where the shot had come from. But, as Simon knew he would be, the arty was too late.

The weapon cracked again. Even in the dusky light Simon saw Niokl's arms go up, heard the muffled scream and the bright tinkle as the knife clattered against a wall. Using the moment, Simon dived for a pile of massive boulders heaped against the wall, and cowered there, his hand going to Daen's dagger in his belt.

He could hear the threshing and kicking as Niokl died a painful, black, lonely death. Twice he cried out to Simon to help him. But the young officer stayed where he was. His only possible chance was that he would be able to outwait Corman and get a chance at him with a knife when the big man moved. To go to the dying arty would simply mean he would be an easy target.

He kept still, kneeling, ready for instant movement.

'Come now, dear Simon. Be sensible. I mean you no harm. I have no wish to tangle with GalSec. Walk with me to talk to that dotard Aenghs, and we can make up a story to please them. What?' Simon waited, feeling his heart pounding against his ribs. 'What do you say? Don't quite trust me yet? Is that it?' Again, the laugh. 'Think I don't know where you are? Here, take this as a small token of my honesty.'

Something slid across the uneven floor towards him, banging against a rock almost at his feet. Cautiously, suspecting a trap of some sort, Simon edged his hand out and touched it.

Instinctively, his fingers jerked back from it. The hot

barrel of a hand-gun. Carefully, fearing a trap, Simon pulled it to him, clasping it firmly by the butt, letting his finger settle on the trigger.

He smiled. Now it was only a matter of time before someone came to his help. In fact he could already hear the pattering of men's feet, running, attracted by the noise.

'Do you really think I'll help you, Corman? After three killings? You must be mad. As soon as the arties get here, I'll tell them what's happened. You're as good as dead.'

The voice that came back to him, rising above the running feet, was calm and gently amused. 'My dear young man. What a sanguine fellow you are, to be sure.'

Then lights showed around the corner, from the cavernous interior of Xoachtl. 'This way. Help! This way!' shouted Simon.

Darkness was pushed back into the shadows and the whole area was filled with armed men, chattering among themselves as soon as they saw the bodies. Cautiously Simon rose to his feet, still holding the gun, looking for Corman.

The leader of the guard party saw Simon first and turned his own weapon on him. Simon smiled, letting the gun point to the floor. 'Don't worry. I'm not the one you want.'

'Oh, but he is. I very much fear that he is.'

His suit crumpled, his face creased with worry, the fat man tiptoed over the loose sand, towards the arties' leader.

Before the man could speak, Corman pointed at Simon. 'There's your villain, Captain. I was coming along here when I saw him hustling my companion along at the point of a blaster. This valiant fellow' – pointing at the shattered corpse of Niokl – 'tried to save him, but he was zapped down. Joel attempted to run, but Rack wasted him. Even while his hands were still tied. If you hadn't come along he would obviously have removed me as the sole witness to his wickedness. I am indebted to you.'

Simon's jaw sagged. The glibness and outrageous nerve of Corman had taken him completely by surprise. All eyes turned to him. Hardly realising what he was doing, he raised the barrel of the gun.

'See; there's the weapon he used.' The light of the arties' torches glinted on Corman's eyes, twinkling amid the rolls of fat.

'No. No, he . . .' Simon stopped as he realised that speech would be wasted. The fat man had tricked him all along the line. It was the weapon that had killed both Joel and Niokl. And there would be only one palm and fingerprint on it. His.

He made his mind up in a flash. The blaster covered the semi-circle of guards. 'No. I'm sorry. He's lying, but I can't prove it.'

Slowly, feeling the ground behind him, Simon backed away. The leader of the arties moved a step towards him, then stopped. 'You have no chance. We can take you at any time.'

'Get back. I don't want to hurt anyone but . . .'

Corman moved forward. 'Apart from unarmed youths! Come, if you will not stop him, then I shall.'

And he began to close with Simon. Biting his lip, he aimed the blaster at the fat man's legs, ready to take up the pressure.

'Come any closer and I'll . . .' he stopped speaking, deterred by a wink from the fat man. Realisation came to him too late.

'All along the line, you fat bastard!' Knowing too well what would happen, he depressed the firing button. There was a faint crackle. Nothing else.

Corman had made sure of all the angles by emptying the blaster after he'd killed Joel and the arty with it.

At the centre of the guards, hands clasped behind his neck, Simon was led back to meet the council. On very different terms from what he'd expected. Corman padded along beside him, breathing heavily, wiping his sweating brow with a large white kerchief. As they walked. Corman talked to him in a low voice.

'Upon my soul, Rack, I didn't think that dear Joel would have betrayed me.'

Not even bothering to look at him, Simon answered him: 'He didn't. I guessed. Daen believed me, and your little sucker butchered her.'

'You guessed! Because you saw me with our little friend back at the Red Hole?'

'Come off that, Corman. Whatever you've told your thinker mates, you're after the treasure here for yourself.'

His shoulders shook at that. 'You may be correct. Not that it will help you at all. But there's treasure and there's treasure.'

Unable to resist, Simon muttered: 'You mean the atica? You'll never get that.'

For the first time Simon felt that Harley Corman was put out. It was obvious that he hadn't guessed that anyone else would know about the priceless drug.

'What do you know of atica?'

Simon kept his lips buttoned together.

'Well. I cannot see how that knowledge will assist you in any way. They will convict you as a killer and that will be the end of it. Poor, poor little Joel. He was such a good . . .' The sentence trailed away into the dimness.

Jabbed by the callousness of the man, Simon turned his head to stare angrily at him. 'My God, Corman! Whatever they'll think, we both know how the poor wretch died. How could you do it?'

Light showed ahead. They were nearly at the council chamber where Simon would be judged.

Quickly Corman whispered his answer to the last question. 'How? My dear fellow, there are plenty of Joels in the galaxy. There is only one supply of atica.'

SIX

A Carpet of Gold

The steel hand that held his brain in a stunning grip seemed to relax a fraction. He was conscious of pain, flowing across the surface of his mind in a myriad barbed ripples.

Cloth tore at his shoulder, slowing up his death fall by a fraction.

A voice calling out to him, sounding higher and more normal. His name recognisable. But the words blurred beyond any comprehension.

The acrid stench of the ammonia lake was stronger in his nostrils. Something yellow flicked at the corner of his eyes. Clothes worn by something else that was falling, far and high above him. Cartwheeling down in frantic, spinning motion.

Time was definitely gaining.

Gaining.

But

it

would

be

too

late.

Too late.

Late.

'Too late to worry about that now, Bogie. It doesn't come down to who's right and who's wrong. Just who's living and who's dead.'

It was still night. Standing by the door of the small

cramped sirque, it was possible to angle your head and peer clean up to the gold-tinted sky, with the Arch of Zayin glowing like some ethereal bridge way above you.

'What time do they kick us out? Didn't Aenghs say at first light?'

Simon turned and sat down, hunching his back against the round wall. By pressing hard it was possible to actually feel the return pressure from the living creature. He yawned, trying to appear unconcerned in front of the older, more experienced man.

'Yes. When the ochre beam splashes against the eye of Xoachtl. That's what he said. That means when the sun lights up that piece of polished stone at the top of the cliffs. Can't be that long now.'

In some ways it was the waiting that Simon had found hard. The talking had been mercifully brief, though Aenghs had been unable to resist the temptation to deliver a moral homily, aimed at him as a triple murderer. He realised that he was, in some ways, getting off lightly.

Bogart seemed to read his mind. 'I tell you, Simon. It could have been a frigging lot worse. I was on some back-side world where killers were heaved into molten glass. Another one where they had their arms and legs surgically removed and then were balanced on a post in the middle of a pool of flesh-eating reptiles.'

Difficult though it was, Simon managed a thin smile. 'Yes. That's a big load of encouragement, Bogie. Still, like you say, while you're running you're still living.'

Outside they could hear the distant shuffling of feet as the arties began to gather to witness their expulsion from Xoachtl. That had been the sentence. Not just for Simon, but for Bogie as well, as his accomplice. To be driven out with no food, no drink and no weapons.

Though Simon still managed to retain the secret of his precious throwing knife.

'I thought the women were going to rip us apart. Don't

95

you reckon it might be worth asking for a private chat with the old man and trying to get him to listen to what really happened? I mean, they ought to be grateful. Instead of kicking us out to die in the backlands.'

They could both hear creaking as men climbed the ladder towards their sirque. It seemed that there was a hint of lightness in the air. Simon looked across at the dim outline of Bogart.

'Hell. It'd have been like trying to argue with T Pyxidis during one of its novas. No, I'm only sorry that I got you into this damned shambles.'

Bogart thumped him lightly on the arm. 'Listen to me. If we're going to go out, and I must say that our chances don't exactly thrill me, then I haven't met many men I'd rather go out with.'

To his surprise Simon found tears pricking his eyes, and he coughed to cover his embarrassment. The curtain was pulled back and armed arties stood there, watching them with a hatred they didn't bother to conceal.

'Come on, you bastards. I only hope one of you twitches without being told. There's nothing I'd like better than to blast you off the side of the cliff.'

Neither man answered. There wasn't an answer to that sort of justified bitterness. Carefully they climbed down the rickety ladders towards the ground, hundreds of metres beneath them.

Simon used a short pause to snatch a look around. Far away, at the edge of sight, a sliver of bright gold was just visible, rising above the horizon. Its yellow rays spread out over the rough landscape, lighting the peaks and deepening the shadows in the valleys.

For a moment his eye was caught by a silvery flash, way over to the south, as though the first rays of the sun had caught some polished metal. It looked like a flying needle.

'Just seen a thinker ship,' he muttered to Bogie. 'Over to the south. Looked as though it might have been landing.'

Bogart didn't answer.

When they got to the bottom, they were surrounded by almost the whole arty colony, angry-faced. There was shouting and a stone was thrown by one of the young men, cutting Bogie's shoulder open. The guards clustered round them and Aenghs called for peace.

He repeated the sentence on them and they were led out to the edge of the community, beyond the bowl-shaped crater. One of the guards pushed them away, nearly making Simon fall on the cruelly-fragmented boulders.

Then they were on their own.

Behind them the rising sun was splashing out from the reflections of the Eye of Xoachtl, teetering at the peak of the cliff.

The sun was barely half-risen; showing as a semi-circle of painful brilliance, it was already getting warm. Both men took a last look back at Xoachtl, with its multi-coloured spheres clinging to the cliffs, linked only by the web of ropes and ladders.

Together they turned back to face the viciously inhospitable desert – one of the worst stretches of terrain in the entire galaxy.

'Which way, Bogie?'

'Not far. Just to get away from that crowd. Then we'll shelter for the hottest part of the day. Travel at night. Make for where you saw that thinkers' ship. Maybe there's a camp there.'

They began to scramble over the splintered rocks towards the south. Trying to avoid falls. Trying to shepherd their strength. Looking for shelter before the sun blazed out and roasted the water from their bodies.

At the back of Simon's mind was one thought; had it been a ship he'd glimpsed? Was there a camp there? If there was, then their sentence of certain death might still be commuted. Like the old sergeant back at the castle had always said : a small hope's a hell of a lot better than no hope at all !

After an hour they seemed to have hardly moved. The sun rose gloriously above them, nearing the lowest point of Zayin's Arch. Sweat was staining both their uniforms, leaving black patches down their chests and over their stomachs. Under both arms and in the small of their backs. The breath rasped harshly in Simon's throat and he already desired water more than anything else in the world.

Anything in the world apart from revenge. Revenge against Corman. The killer with the knife beneath the cloak. The smiler.

The salt stung his eyes, prickling his skin, bringing the old sores out again, as though they'd never healed. They came to a level part, in soft sand along the bed of what must once have been a flowing torrent. Eyes closed, Simon trudged mechanically along, torturing himself with thoughts of what it must once have been. Ice-cold waters flowing over his feet. Cool liquid bubbling across smoothed stones.

Not caring where his feet went, he stumbled and fell, jarring his ribs painfully.

The blow to his ribs jarred him painfully. He felt his shoulder-strap catch on something, slowing down his descent. Breath hard in his chest. The biting of the ammonia far stronger than it had been.

The cave was small and cramped, but it kept the worst heat of the sun out, and it saved some of the water in their bodies from evaporating. They'd been there for most of the day and it was nearly time to go again.

They hadn't talked much – there really wasn't much to say. If there was a camp somewhere out there, then they could tackle that as it came. If there wasn't, then they'd probably be dead in between two or three days. If they'd aimed for either Fort Peine or Fort Dure as soon as they were expelled from Xoachtl, then they might have had an outside chance of reaching it.

If they had, they'd have been arrested or maybe murdered. Either way there wouldn't have been anything they could do to get back at Harley Corman. And, coincidentally, help the arties. But that motive came way down the list in second place.

Bogart had used some of the sweltering day talking about survival. Simon had gone through the approved courses, but he had found early on that there was a mile of difference between theory and practice.

Cool lecturers and taking notes in heated or air-conditioned rooms.

Dying with your black tongue swollen to fill your ulcerated mouth.

'Perspire as little as possible and suck something. Raw onion is one of the best things for this. Half a gallon of water is needed to work adequately in a cool climate. Double that in heat.'

That was what the manual said. There wasn't any raw anything to suck on. No smooth pebbles. Just gritty shards of splintered sand.

It was difficult not to perspire when sweat dripped off the end of your nose just sitting in the shade trying hard not to move a muscle.

'Must have a piss. Hey, Bogie!'

'What?'

'Why can't we drink it? Better than nothing. Filter it in some way.'

Bogart's voice was weary. 'Listen, young Simon. Piss is salty. That makes you thirsty. That doesn't seem a good idea to me. Eh?' Simon looked so disconsolate that Bogart grinned painfully. 'But if you soak your tunic in it and rub it all over your body, it helps preserve some of your body liquid.'

Although he'd been prepared to drink it, Simon found himself oddly squeamish at the idea of rubbing it on his skin. Only when Bogart took the lead did he follow suit. He found the cooling effect, though brief, of some sort of relief.

Throughout that day Simon had continually been impressed by Bogie's knowledge of survival techniques. When the rays of the sun had blistered the skin on his face, and he'd started taking off his uniform top, Bogart had stopped him, pointing out the necessity of checking the evaporation of sweat.

'Bogie, without you I'd never have made it. Thanks.'

His comrade wasted precious moisture trying to spit. 'Listen, Simon. Being half of a team means never having to say thanks. Hey, I love that. Might make part of a story.'

As soon as the sun had dropped near the broken horizon, they started off again. Simon had been careful to take a mental bearing of where the thinkers' ship had descended, and they headed for it on as true a bearing as they could.

The rocks were still too hot to touch with comfort, but they gradually cooled as evening strode towards them out of the blackness. Fortunately the glow of the space rubbish, like a radio-active rainbow, was enough for them to travel by. Zayin had no moon.

It was difficult over that terrain to estimate how far had been travelled, but Bogie reckoned that they'd covered around a third of their target distance.

It was near dawn that Bogart fell into the bottomless crevasse. One moment he had been leading the way, his heavy panting acting as a guide for Simon, trailing along a few metres behind. Next moment there had been a croaking yell and the clattering of disturbed stones sliding down into an echoing void.

'Bogie! Christ! Bogie!!'

The cascading boulders rattled and rang, the noise seeming to go on for an eternity. At last there was silence. Disregarding the needles of stone that dug into his arms and chest, Simon flung himself full-length on the edge of the crack in the earth, trying to look down.

The light was so dim that he could barely see further than the end of his arm. Twice he shouted for Bogart, straining to hear a reply from the bottom of those plumbless depths.

When a voice answered him, he was shocked that it came from so close. Maybe three or four metres below. Faint and shaky.

'Here. There's a ledge. Half a metre wide and about two long. Feels as crumbly as hell. I'm trying to stand up on it.'

There was the noise of more earth and stone shifting and falling. Simon tried counting to guess how deep the hole was.

He gave up at forty.

That was entirely too deep.

At last he could just make out the white circle of Bogie's face, swimming as far as he could see, like a drowned moon in a pit of blackness.

Reaching down as far as possible, Simon realised that he was still short. Quickly he stripped off his standard issue belt and tried with that.

'No good. I miss it by a couple of hands' breadths. Wait on. I'll take off my belt and throw it up to you. You can put them together and haul me up.' A pause. 'Better be a bit smartish, young Simon. This ledge won't see me through the night.'

More shufflings, then a grunt of effort as Bogie threw the belt. But the rocks were jagged and there was a slight overhang. It snagged and fell back into the crack. Simon shut his eyes, thinking all was lost.

'Simon. I caught it. But I might not next time. Your turn to come up with a bright idea. Hey! What the frigging burning . . . No ! !'

With a wriggle and a swing, Simon was on the ledge with

him. They both felt it sway, and dip another few centimetres. Then it was still.

His voice pitched low, Bogart spoke : 'In my years in the service, I've seen some stupid gravs. Some colossally stupid showers of green dreck. But you, Simon Kennedy Rack, are without any doubt the most . . .'

Simon interrupted him : 'No time for compliments, old friend. This ledge isn't big enough for the both of us. Here's my belt. Hold both of them in your teeth and climb up on my shoulders. Then you can lower them and pull me out. Otherwise, if we lose one of them, you're rotten meat in the bowels of this crapulous world.'

In the heavy silence they both heard the distant hum of a needle ship's reversing thrust as it came in for a landing not that far away.

Trying to assume a voice of sweet reason, Bogart was ready to argue. Simon stopped him. 'Listen, you tub of drive grease. Get up before I kick your arse through your ugly face ! Right?'

'Yes, sir,' said Bogie, unable to keep the amusement from his voice.

Another shift in the ledge speeded him up. Carefully he climbed up on Simon's shoulders, the belts swinging wildly in his teeth. The stones beneath Simon's feet creaked and groaned. There was a spring and the load was gone from his shoulders.

It only took a moment for Bogart to lower the lifeline to him and he scrambled up to safety, lying panting beside Bogart.

In the finest fiction the ledge would have given way at that very moment and roared into the deeps. Life's not always like that !

They stood up, both noticing the first rays of the next day's sun lightening the sky. Bogart simply clasped Simon's hand. 'Rack. If we struggle out of this mess with our skins intact, and GalSec receives us back to its bosom, I would be delighted to find that chance had allocated you to me as a partner.'

'In scout ships?'

Bogie grinned broadly. 'That's the way I want to go. I'm pissed off right up to here with being smothered in a starship. It's the open space for me.'

They shook hands on it.

The rest during the hottest part of the day helped their health, but they still looked like a couple of long-buried skeletons. Haggard-faced and covered in dust and sand.

Quickly, for the sun was beginning to bake them, they searched for shelter. They found a hollow. Not so good as the previous day, but passable in keeping them in some shade.

They huddled in it, both trying to get some sleep.

Suddenly Bogart chuckled.

'What's the matter?'

'I was just thinking of an old song. What I felt when you suddenly cascaded out of the blackness and landed by me on that rickety ledge. When you grabbed me.'

'What bloody song?'

'Something about : the first time ever you held my hand. I felt the earth move.'

Since Simon hadn't the faintest idea what he was on about, Bogie's attempted joke fell flat.

During the day it was hard to sleep because of the extreme heat, but both men dropped into occasional dozing, waking with a start.

Nothing moved in all the backlands that day, apart from a heavy rumble of rocks somewhere near them. As it wasn't repeated, they decided it must have been the ledge giving way.

Which it was.

The dazzling yellow light seemed to burn its way through closed eyes right into your mind.

Above him Simon saw another body crashing down towards him, arms and legs flailing like a disjointed puppet. There was a mist swirling round its chest and head that puzzled him. Until he realised that its pink aura must be blood.

So Bogie got him.

'The old team. Never fails,' he muttered as he slid more and more slowly towards the lake.

When it was time to go on, Simon found himself feeling immeasurably weary. The skin on his face was cracked and peeling, with ulcerated sores at the corners of his mouth. His eyes pained him and his knee and shoulder joints ached. His teeth felt loose in their sockets and his tongue was still swollen. They had both tried to pass water to bathe their skins, but neither had been able to manage more than a few strongly-coloured drops.

But they had to go on.

The needle-ship of the thinkers had landed, but neither of them had heard it take off again. So it had to be still around.

In that massive desert the shining metal should have stood out like a pig on ice. But there was no sign of it.

'Must be in a ravine close by. Problem is, where?'

They trudged on, slipping and falling. They had become so hardened that they didn't even bother to curse any more when they tumbled over some jagged outcrop. Their uniforms were torn and filthy, with blood speckling their bodies.

Their feet were a mass of bloody blisters and their hands badly cut and grazed. During that night they covered barely half the distance they'd managed the first night.

As the sun crept out to start its day's travel, they collapsed in a small hollow giving the most minimal shade. Although neither mentioned it, both knew that if they didn't find a camp early on the next night, they would have reached the limits of their endurance.

At least it was easier to sleep in their totally exhausted state. The shaking of the earth woke Simon first, rattling Bogie into alertness moments later. A deep, thundering noise, with the overriding whine of a ram engine on full lift.

Its pointed nose tearing through the sky like a scalpel through flesh, the thinkers' ship blasted by them, the wind of its passing making them cower down and cover their eyes against the tearing hail of grit and small pebbles.

After the buffeting had passed, Bogie touched Simon on the shoulder. 'Great! That can't have been more than a mile away. We'll be at their camp well before midnight.'

But Simon didn't share his enthusiasm. 'There's a big "If" about that, Bogie.'

'What d'you mean?'

'Suppose that ship was taking them *all* off. When we get to the camp, we find a circle of scorched sand and damn-all else.'

The rest of the day was spent in near silence.

Once most of the molten disc had sunk beneath the far horizon, they began their move. Despite their exhaustion and the appalling terrain, they made good speed, hardly noticing any new cuts and bruises in their rush to get to where the ship had blasted off.

When they found it, they realised why they hadn't been able to see it from any distance. The camp was in another crater. Smaller than the one in front of Xoachtl, but deep enough to hide a flotilla of needle ships. At the bottom of it they could see small bubbles of temporary dwellings, each with its own heating and liquefaction plant.

'None of them have got anyone in. Look; there's no light showing in any of them. It's fucking deserted!!'

Simon almost wept in his disappointment. They were too late. The ship must have blasted off with the thinkers on board, taking them the short hop to Xoachtl, where it would probably put them down on floaters.

'Look!' Bogart counted hurriedly. 'Six in from the right. There's a dim light there. Come on.'

There was the sound of a low-drive electric utility motor humming away in the lit hut, muted by the insulation on roof and walls. Placing each foot carefully and quietly in front of the other, Bogie and Simon made their way cautiously forward.

Armed with a couple of hunks of jagged rock, Bogart took the front, while Simon crept towards the back. The only light was the ghostly phosphorescence of the Arch.

Feeling the roughness of the stones bite into his sore hands, Bogie went forward at a slow crouch. For a moment he paused as the humming note changed in pitch then resumed its previous steady drone.

He was within twenty paces.

'Drop the stones and rise to your feet.'

The voice was cold and metallic, echoing and inhuman. He spun round, arm cocked for a throw, when a beam of light flashed out, hurling him back on the ground. There was a searing pain in his shoulder and a numbness in the muscles of his arms.

'Stupid fool. Now I wish to know who you are and what you are doing here. If you do not tell me, I will blast your mind so that you can never again make your trivial arty productions.'

The voice was unflustered and impersonal. In the dim darkness Bogie could just see who it came from. Floating a metre in the air, on a silvery platform, sat a thinker, grotesque in his exoskeleton. A weapon of some sort was pointed at Bogie.

Behind the hut Simon had frozen at the voice and peered warily round the corner. From where he was, it was clear that the thinker was alone. And he had a floater. With its anti-grav device it was just what they wanted to get them back to Xoachtl and destroy Harley Corman. It would carry two at a pinch, and it would drift them over any of the arties' defences.

But the thinker had Bogie at his mercy. He was armed and armoured. Quickly he whipped out his knife and started to slash strips from his uniform top.

Time. Bogie knew Simon would try and save him. If he had time. 'What makes you think I'm an artie?'

'I am the one who asks the questions. It is obvious to me that you are arty filth. What else could you be?'

Pretending he was worse than he was, Bogart stalled for time by groaning and holding his head. 'I suppose you're right.'

'Of course. We have studied your pathetic colony for many years. I know every arty fact there is to know.'

'Every artefact about what?'

'What? About what?'

'What artefacts?'

'All arty facts.'

'Where from?' Bogart was almost beginning to enjoy this absurd game. And it was buying time.

'Where? How can you say "where" about facts about arties?'

'Oh! Those arty facts. Not artefacts?'

The head, a tiny ball in its enveloping powered armour shook at him. 'You waste my time with your idle chatter. By the setting of the sun tomorrow your whole putrid colony will be a shadow of a memory.'

The floater came gently to earth, landing with a barely audible crunch on the sand. Stretching like some hideously animated insect, the thinker stretched his long legs and rose to a standing position, topping Bogart by nearly half a metre.

'I think you must be only a miserable spy. I cannot think you are in a position to harm us. So logic simply tells me that I must kill you.'

There was the faintest whistle of a missile, and the clunk

of it striking home. Slowly, like some scaffolded building being demolished, the thinker crashed to the rocks. As he fell, his finger tightened on the firing button of his weapon, and a stream of light blasted a huge boulder to a spray of shards.

There was the tinkle of the blaster slipping from unconscious fingers. Then a giggle.

'God, Bogie, that chat about artefacts had me bursting trying not to laugh. Still, it gave me the time I wanted.'

Bogart stepped over to where the thinker lay stretched out, and looked down at him. The light from the nearby hut was bright enough to see the thread of blood that trickled down the side of the tiny man's face.

'How d'you do that? Throw a stone at him?'

'No. Too risky. When we were kids at the castle, we used to go wildfowling with slings and stones. I managed to make a quick sling out of strips of my uniform and hurled a pebble at him with it. Nasty little sod. Serve him right.'

They didn't even waste time on tying up the thinker. The floater was their first concern. It wasn't damaged, and both men knew enough of the principles involved to be able to pilot it.

While Bogie checked the drive level, Simon climbed aboard it. 'With this we'll be at Xoachtl easily by dawn. Then we can get things moving for Corman.'

'What about him? Maybe he's got a coder?' He paused. 'Simon, I think it'd be safer to out him. Don't you?'

Simon hesitated. If anyone had suggested to him seven days ago in one of the midmen's messes that in a week's time he would be standing there, his uniform in rags, cut and bleeding, deciding whether to murder a man in cold blood, he'd have laughed. Now it wasn't funny.

In some ways he was lucky. The thinker made the decision for him by returning to consciousness. With the hissing of air in joints, he levered himself up to his full height and strode towards them.

'Murdering killers. You'd have left me to die in this un-speakable wilderness. For that you must . . .'

Bogart shut him up by heaving a vast boulder at his spidery legs, knocking him to the ground again. Simon jumped off the floater to help his comrade, but the thinker was quickly up again, his right leg trailing and bent. His eyes flicked from one to the other.

Suddenly, like some supercharged ballet-dancer, the thinker whirled on his good leg and lashed out with an elongating arm. It had sprouted a needle-tipped spike, and it slashed through the air at Simon. Gasping at the speed of it, he was only saved by the pale glint of light off the metal. Instinctively, he dived on his back and the blade missed him. But it came close enough for the wind of its passing to raise gooseflesh.

Bogart darted in behind the blow, another chunk of rock clenched in his fist. Using a short, powerful jab, he struck at the delicate knee-joint of the exo. There was a harsh grinding of gears locking, and the towering thinker toppled and nearly fell. The straight leg had locked, and the whole framework tipped sideways at a crazy angle.

'Perdition ! Whore's-spawn ! !'

It was a mistake to think that the exo was totally crippled, as Bogie found out to his cost. Before he could move back, a cracking blow from the powerful right hand nearly sent him to the promised land. A black curtain dropped over his eyes and he was vaguely aware of the stickiness of blood on his face.

Awkwardly, the thinker pivoted, the right arm arcing up and back, ready to scythe down on the helpless officer. Simon jumped forward, watching warily for the counter blow against him. When it came whistling down he did the unexpected. Instead of trying to duck it, he leaped over it, clinging like a sirque to the exo. His toes scrabbled for a hold on the framework, and his hands reached up for the vulner-able head of the thinker.

Like two matadors playing a lethal bull, the two men circled and tormented the staggering thinker. For all the strength and power of his exo, he was gradually being worn down and defeated. While Simon climbed higher, ducking inside the windmilling arms, Bogie hopped about down below, heaving stones at the weakened legs.

A flailing elbow caught Simon an agonising crack in the ribs, but he was in reach of the thinker, vulnerable, like the yolk of an egg outside its shell. He swung a fist, and had the ineffable pleasure of feeling it pulp home in the centre of their enemy's face, spreading bloody bone under his knuckles.

The thinker emitted a thin scream, and the arms shot up in the air, momentarily out of control. Bogart didn't miss his chance and shoulder-charged the legs. There was a moment when it seemed the thinker would recover, but the strained durstel of the legs buckled and cracked. Simon jumped clear at the last second as the exo fell to the rocks. The scream was cut off short.

As the top of the exo hit the jagged boulders, there was a clattering of metal. And a soft, wet thud, like an apple being dropped on a stone floor. The lower half of the exo-skeleton completely disintegrated and rolled crookedly away, leaving the corpse of the thinker trapped in the useless top half.

Rubbing his bruised chest, Simon got slowly to his feet and walked over to where Bogie was looking thoughtfully down at the remains of their diminutive opponent.

'Christ, Bogie. He isn't very big without all his aids, is he?'

Bogart grinned, wiping away the film of blood from his battered face. 'Nope. In fact, you could say he's not half the man he used to be.'

SEVEN

The City's Melted Furnace

At last movement seemed to have stopped. The fingers of his left hand were wet and burned. It took a vast effort of will, but Commander Simon Rack succeeded in pulling his hand away from the stinging liquid.

The stench of ammonia was so strong in his nostrils that he nearly choked. He knew that he had to get away, but that involved an even greater effort, and he didn't think he was quite up to that.

He opened his eyes.

Hanging over him, seeming suspended in space, was the dark face and torn body of the mad killer, Ahmed. The one eye that remained was open and staring. Where the other had been was a black pool of blood.

It was an odd, frozen moment of crystalline time.

The red blood dropped infinitely slowly to the scrubby yellow grass, splattering in slow-motion on the red-brown earth.

Bogart cursed quietly, fluently and endlessly as he tried to stop the blood trickling from the cut on his head. It fell in regular spots to the parched red-brown earth just below the floater.

The muttering had been going on ever since they had got away from the thinkers' camp and looked like continuing all the way to Xoachtl. Midman Rack had become used to it, and concentrated all his energy on piloting the tricky machine. It had been designed for one thinker, including his heavy exo. Two solidly-built GalSec officers weighed rather more, and the bottom of the floater only just skimmed over the needle peaks of rock.

The cursing finally ceased. 'Stopped the sod. I thought he must have leaked some anti-clotting stuff out of his exo. How much further? It must be close to dawn now. Look up there.'

There was a golden glow filling the sky, brightening the whole land. But the centre of the arties was close. The crater where they'd been stopped by the hally was just in front of them – about half a mile.

'We'll be in time to warn the arties,' said Simon exultantly.

At that precise moment, showing a nice taste in dramatic irony, the floater tipped sharply to the earth. Both men were flung sharply forward, landing in a heap in a small hollow.

'My frigging bow's bent!'

Simon didn't reply. The crack on his head from Bogie's bony knee had stunned him, and he was waiting for his mind to come crawling back to him. Bogart's bow wasn't the first thing he wanted to worry about. Though the weapons that Bogart managed to manufacture out of the shattered remnants of the exoskeleton might save their lives.

The main support struts – those that weren't broken – supplied the bows, and the arrows were the lighter members, snapped off, and filed roughly down to a point. The bowstrings came from the artificial gut tendons that carried the power to the limbs of the aid. The arrows were flightless, but they would serve at short range.

While Bogie wrestled with his bow, Simon retrieved his weapons from the sand. The failure of the floater was a sore blow to them. They knew that the attack of the thinkers on Xoachtl, aided by the treachery of Harley Corman within the fortress, was due to begin shortly. Now they were faced with a hard slog across the desert under the rising sun, with the probability of being spotted by either the arties or the thinkers. Or both. And possibly being blanked out by the arties' hallucinogenic defences.

'We can't risk going in the front way, Simon. I don't want to arrive for the fight with my mind oozing out of my ears.'

'Right. That means cutting round . . .' he paused, weighing up the options open to them, 'that way. Left. And trying to come in under the lee of the cliff. Under that colony of sirques up there.'

Just as the light of the sun splashed on the polished stone Eye of Xoachtl, there was an explosion from the base of the mesa. Smoke billowed up, swirling in the pale glow of morning. They could hear screams and just make out figures scurrying about the main entrance to the fortress.

'It's started, Bogie. Come on.'

At full stretch, dodging among the scant cover, it took them nearly an hour to get to their objective. Simon thought as they hurried across the cruel land that it wouldn't have been possible if they hadn't found a small store of food and water at the thinkers' camp. In the excitement of impending action, both of them forgot all their cuts and bruises and tiredness.

They finally reached the shadow of the cliff undetected, with the brightly-painted sirques hanging above them, fixed to the naked rock. Just ahead of them they could see the giant forms of a group of thinkers, entrenched behind a barricade of boulders, firing at a smaller number of arties. The thinkers were in much the better position, and were picking off their enemies at their leisure.

'They haven't got a chance. Corman must have sabotaged their defences. Look at all the arties' bodies by the Water Gate. We've got to get past this lot.'

Bogart suddenly pointed up above them, and unslung his makeshift bow. Simon looked where he was pointing. Directly over the position of the thinkers was a cluster of sirques, their colours burning in the flame-bright light.

There was a fair amount of smoke billowing about them, and Simon could see that some of them were shifting uneasily.

'See. They don't like all this noise and killings and fumes. It shouldn't be that hard to make them move in a big way.'

Gritting his teeth, Bogie bent his bow, followed by Simon. The durstel struts were immensely strong, and should, in theory, project the arrows with great force. Bogie pointed at one spherical dwelling, about a hundred feet up the cliff, that was already moving a little. 'The one with the red clouds on it. Draw. Aim. Loose.'

Archery had been an essential art at Castle Falcon, and Simon found he hadn't lost his skill. His shaft flew amazingly true, burying itself in the soft skin of the sirque. Bogie had underestimated the power of his bow, but he had a lucky break as his arrow flew on to strike another sirque forty feet higher.

Afterwards neither man could swear to it, but both felt rather than heard a deep sonorous note as the arrows bit. One of the thinkers also glanced upwards, as though something had distracted him. There was a shower of sand and a few small pebbles, and more of the thinkers looked up in alarm, suspecting that some of the arties had managed to get above them.

'Again,' said Simon urgently, and two more arrows found targets, vanishing into the pulpy flesh of the sirques with the power of the bows.

One of the thinkers stood up and shouted out, pointing up at the cliff and back at where Simon and Bogart hid. In his exo he was silhouetted blackly against the rising sun, and he was too easy a victim for the survivors among the arties. Three streams from blasters hit him, spreading him all over his comrades and the surrounding rocks.

But, above on the cliffs, it was all happening. Three of the four sirques were moving, faster than anyone would have believed possible for their bulk. Two more arrows shifted another of them.

There was a scream from the thinkers. Pebbles and larger rocks were now cascading down the orange cliff, landing among them. Bogart was preparing to fire another arrow, when Simon touched his arm.

'No need. Look!'

One of the sirques was falling. A clear liquid oozed from where the arrows had hit it, blurring the pretty patterns. With a heavy thud that shook the area, it smashed down, missing the main group of thinkers by a narrow margin. More boulders were falling, some coming close to where Bogart and Simon hid.

Then, what they'd aimed for. The first sirque they'd hit also fell, followed almost immediately by another, turning like monstrous balls as they toppled, the colours on their vast sides streaking into each other like a fearful kaleidoscope.

They hit the thinkers, grinding them all into the bare rock. There was a fountain of dust, and a single agonised scream that faded slowly away, echoing back off the cliffs. After that there was silence.

The arties who'd been pinned down by the thinkers took one look at what had happened and scampered off towards the main gate, without bothering to see who or what had produced the miracle that had saved their lives. Shaking dust from their clothes, Simon and Bogie followed them at a more leisurely pace.

When they reached the main entrance to Xoachtl, the Water Gate, they found a scene of dreadful slaughter, with bodies everywhere. It was obvious that the brunt of the first attack had come here, and dozens of arties had paid the ultimate price for trying to bar entrance to the thinkers.

'Why were the main gates open, anyway?' asked Bogart, of nobody in particular.

Simon glanced around. They seemed to be the only living people for some distance. Further into the fortress there was the muted sound of fighting, and noxious fumes belched out along the corridors. He noticed that there were far fewer dead from the scientists' side than from the artists', which spoke of treachery.

A groan from the shadowed wall attracted their attention. Lying in a sticky pool of his own blood, one of the arties was still alive, his left leg ending in a jagged string of gristle and white bone. Simon eased him up and wiped the dirt from his face. The eyes opened, but there was no recognition in them. Only the blank knowledge of approaching death.

The voice was frail and hollow; so weak that it seemed a breath of wind would take it away for ever. 'Treachery ... we were on guard at dawn ... The fat man ... two of us came and stabbed us ... cowards!' A coughing fit overtook him and blood dribbled down his chin. Simon glanced up at Bogie, who shook his head. Rallying briefly, the arty went on: 'I am called Elsbarg. The guard on the Water Gate ... Those running dogs ... Erlik and Halda betrayed us ... Now the thinkers are all in the fortress ... Xoachtl has fallen.'

Tears trickled through the dust and blood on his face, splashing on his naked body. He groaned and squeezed at Simon's hand. 'My leg hurts very ...'

His head went slack on his shoulders and the fingers relaxed. Simon put the body down and stood up, absently wiping blood from his fingers on his tattered uniform.

'So.' The monosyllable was flat. Almost a question. Bogart looked back at him and shrugged his shoulders.

Simon took his bow from across his shoulders and notched an arrow, ready for use. 'We go in. Yes?'

Bogart grinned, grimacing as the gesture cracked open the sores on his face and round his mouth. 'Yes. Why not?'

Simon led the way, stepping over the bodies heaped by

the Water Gate, now a place of silence and death. 'Let's get away from here. It really bugs me.'

The corpses were thickly clustered at every turn of the corridor. At first they were mainly arties, but the balance was gradually restored as the defenders had got themselves better organised after the first stunning shock of the betrayal.

'Simon,' whispered Bogie, as they drew nearer to the noisy scene of the fighting. 'I don't get it. If Corman wanted his mates to win here, and he's as good as we both reckon he is, then why didn't he do a better job on letting them in? I reckon he could have timed it a lot better to give them a chance to take it with hardly any fighting.'

Simon stopped. In the corridor it was nearly dark, with the light tubes guttering and flickering. The main power supply to Xoachtl was in jeopardy from the attack. 'Bogie, haven't you tumbled it yet? Corman is after himself and nobody else. The thinkers were just to give him the diversion. He's risking two sects on a dying planet to get his hands on the treasures and on the atica. He doesn't give a single flying fuck about the thinkers.'

There was the crump of a powerful explosion from round the corner, and the blast threw them both back against the wall. Simon found himself feeling light-headed, and tried to breathe shallowly. 'Hally gas, Bogie. Watch it. That's why those thinkers the sirques crushed had breathers on. Corman'd tipped them off.'

Fortunately it was only a passing cloud, and its effects were soon dissipated. An arty, his eyes staring wildly and babbling to himself, went staggering past, favouring them with a pleasant grin as he did so. He was spaced way out, and was totally and mercifully unaware that coils of yellow intestine were sliding greasily out of a deep cut across his bare stomach.

The centre of the fighting was the council chamber, with

its superbly painted vaulted roof, and its row upon row of carved seats. The next turning in the winding pathway showed a scene of carnage. Simon saw what was happening at a glance.

The arties had chosen to make their stand there, and each tier had its defenders, seemingly prepared to die for their homes. The thinkers, although protected to some extent by their exoskeletons, were paying dearly for each metre they gained. At a quick count, it looked as though there were already well over a hundred dead and dying in that one room.

Bogart put his lips close to Simon's ear so that nothing would draw attention to them. 'We'll never get through there. Anyway, I reckon that Corman'll be elsewhere by now. We've got to find the atica chambers.'

Simon nodded. 'Kay. Look! Over there. By that pillar. Isn't that Hualpa?'

The arty who'd shown them a degree of friendship in their brief stay in Xoachtl. With a few young men round him, he was desperately trying to consolidate a position and take the main force of thinkers from the flank. Simon stood up, exposing himself riskily to the shots of both sides, and waved to the arty. His face begrimed and strained, the man saw him and waved puzzledly back.

Frantically Simon motioned to him to join them, and the arty finally did so, dodging several wildly-aimed shots at him. He was panting and shaking. Partly with anger and partly with fright.

To their relief, he didn't seem at all surprised to see them back from the wilderness, accepting their presence as just one of the happenings of a mind-toppling day. Under Simon's brief questioning, Hualpa told them what had happened.

Corman had got two of the arties to betray their fellows, and slay the guards on Water Gate. The thinkers had rushed in and gained easy access. But then the resistance had stiffened and they were just holding them in a stalemate position in the huge central chamber. The thinkers couldn't go further forward, and the arties wouldn't retreat. They were all prepared to die where they were.

'How many of your people are left?'

Hualpa quickly reckoned on his fingers. 'I think less than half.'

Simon whistled. If the fighting went on much longer then both communities would be devastated. It was part of his function as a GalSec operative to stop the mutual massacre as soon as possible. He thought about it for a second and then pushed the idea to a small room way back in his mind and shut the door firmly on it.

'Where's Corman?'

Hualpa peered round through the smoke and fumes and shook his head. 'I haven't seen him for some time. In fact I haven't seen Corman himself at all. I saw Erlik and Halda going towards the . . .' He stopped, his face betraying his sudden anxiety.

'Towards the atica and treasure chambers? Come on, Hualpa. If we're to help at all we've got to get there. Take us.'

There was a moment of agonising tension. To betray the deepest secrets of his people to strangers. Men who had been cast out into the backlands and who had come back alive. This struck at the roots of his being.

Bogart grabbed him by the scruff of the neck and shook him like a half-drowned dog. 'Come on. By the power vested in me as an officer of the Galactic Security Service of the Federation, I command you to tell me.' He dropped the pitch of his voice to a confidential whisper. 'If you don't I'll break your knees and elbows so you never walk or paint anything again.'

Either of the threats might have worked. One of them did. With a last glance at his comrades, locked in the death struggle with their bitter enemies, Hualpa led them back, branching off down a narrower side corridor.

From there they plunged into a labyrinth of dim passages, sometimes sloping upwards and sometimes down. The illustrations on the wall grew cruder, and there was a growing feeling of antiquity.

They stopped in front of an immense door of some heavy metal, and Hualpa turned to them, his face bewildered in the faint lighting.

'What's wrong?'

'The gate of knowledge. It has never been left unguarded in all the centuries that Xoachtl has been our home. Beyond it lies what the wicked man requires. And, look, it is open!!'

It was true. The door stood ajar, the light flickering over the snakes and dragons that ornamented the panels on its facing. Beyond it there was an absolute darkness. Simon laid his hand on the door, finding that it was perfectly balanced, despite its vast weight. At that moment they heard an eerie moaning from the stygian blackness.

Hualpa clutched his arm in a passion of terror. 'Listen. What has been disturbed?'

Again the cry came to their ears. Quieter now. And a third time. Simon heaved the door open and rushed in.

'That's no monster; it's a man. Wounded. Flames of Hell! I can't see a thing in here. I think ... Here!'

He had stumbled over something lying sprawled on the gritty flagstones. Something that wriggled and moaned under his feet. Bogie found some ancient lamps hanging behind the door, and turned the pale yellow beam on the floor.

The past few days had hardened Simon Rack. He wasn't the boy he'd been in Fort Peine. That boy had seen things and experienced aspects of life in his early years that would have sent many strong men mewling to a quiet room and a pile of soft blankets where they could bury their mind. But that was before.

Now his mind and body had been toughened to new and

unknowable limits. What he saw there sickened him beyond normal tolerance, but he could look on it, and act.

The thing that had cried out had once been the leader of the artists' community on Zayin, the elder Aenghs. Both eyes had been plucked from their sockets. His face was such a mask of drying blood that it was difficult to see what had been done. His lips seemed to have been peeled away from his mouth, and his cheeks resembled a slaughterer's lacework of cuts and torn flesh.

Hualpa fell to his knees and wept at the sight, his shoulders shaking. Bogart spat philosophically in the dust. The hands, feet and genitals had been wickedly mutilated, and most of the major joints dislocated. It was a miracle that he still breathed. He felt Simon touch him gently, and he moaned and tried, dying as he was, to crawl away.

'It is me, Aenghs. Simon Rack. I have come to take vengeance on the men who did this to you. You must tell me where they are.'

Hualpa shouted out so that his voice bounced and reechoed through the darkness, finally vanishing in the thick velvet dust. 'It was Corman. I will tear the heart from his living body for this. Hualpa speaks ! ! !'

'No.' The voice was amazingly strong. 'It was not Corman who did this to me. Not Corman. He came later, after it was done. And he cursed those who had done it for their cruelty to me. It was a thinker. Called Fara. And' – the voice weakened for the first time – 'two of our people. Erlik and Halda.'

Simon had looked up at Bogie when the mention of the thinker's name came. Fara. The thinker from the Red Hole. His eyes cold and distant, he looked down at the old man.

'They were after the secret of the atica and the treasure?'

The mangled head nodded once. 'I told them. I could not do other than that. The pain took my mind from me. But I did not tell them all. I told them of the pathway.' His voice became an odd sing-song chant, like a child repeating a well-learned lesson. 'Twice to right and then to left. Three from where you are to left. Then the right fork. That is what I told them.'

Simon clenched his fingers into the palms of his hands. Corman had only three with him. A thinker and two arties. Now was the time to take him. Before he had a chance to get away. He repeated the instructions to himself. 'Twice right and one left. Three from where you are to left. I suppose that's where a lot of tunnels meet. Right fork after that. Got it. But, Aenghs. Can you hear me?'

The face had begun to relax. Already Simon could see the signs that the soul and the body were about to be parted. He repeated his question. Fresh blood bubbled up from the old man's chest and he smiled through his broken mouth.

'I hear the tinkling of water in a quiet pool. I hear the wind moving a pebble where sun and sky meet. I hear the footfall of a fresh maiden in a cool meadow. I hear you, Simon Rack.'

'What did you not tell them?'

'Oh, just a small thing. What a warm welcome they will get down there. Eh?' He began to giggle to himself. Quietly, growing louder. Laughing until his whole frame shook. Enjoying the jest that he was to take with him. For his tortured body couldn't stand the extra strain. With no warning, he stiffened and shook as though he had an ague. His arms and legs flailed for a moment, uncontrollably. Just as suddenly, he became still.

Hualpa sighed, once more under control. 'Farewell, Aenghs. I think that Xoachtl is doomed and your death is only one of many. And the many make a whole.'

Bogart grunted. 'Simon, this isn't the time for all this mystic crap. Let's go after them. We've got the instructions. We can catch them if we hurry. Corman's too fat to go very quickly down here.'

''Kay. Just that I'm worried about the trap. Obviously there must be something to protect the stuff down there.

Probably passed down from chief to chief. Still, the general never won the battle by waiting to wipe his ass. We'll have to be careful. I'll go first with the light. Then Hualpa, then you. Right?'

For a second Simon was certain Bogart was going to argue with him, but he thought better of it. They set off into the deepest stages of the buried maze under the red rocks of Xoachtl.

The first turning they came to, Simon led them right, and again at the second turn. The left turn was a narrow crack that they could easily have missed, then came a wide space, where at least a dozen passages converged. Carefully, Simon counted three round to the left, and they carried on.

Far beneath the massive cliffs, they were conscious of the depth and weight of all that stone, seeming to press down on them. Huapa had the fear of superstition on his shoulders. But for the two officers, used to limitless vistas of space, the ordeal was a thousand times worse. Despite the cold and dampness, Simon found himself sweating profusely.

They all halted when there was an echo below them. For nearly an hour they had heard nothing but their own feet padding softly over the stones. Simon had ordered complete silence in case their enemies heard them coming and ambushed them from one of the numerous side turnings. So the noise had to be Corman's party.

'What in the name of . . . ?'

'Sounded like someone's just found out what old Aenghs was laughing at.'

Simon moved forward again. 'Yes. Teach us to be extra careful.'

The air still seemed to vibrate with that awful choking short scream. They finally reached the clear fork that Aenghs had mentioned. Holding the light before him, Simon took the right-hand passage.

Another couple of hundred metres, and Bogart stopped, sniffing. 'Simon, I'm suffering from hally again. I can smell roasting meat.'

Simon stopped by him and inhaled deeply. 'You're right, Bogie. How the ... come on. Careful.'

Round another winding bend and the air was pungent with smoke and the smell of burned flesh. Simon tried to wave the smoke away, but it hung in the corridor, wrapping itself familiarly about their legs, and irritating the surface of their eyes.

It was Hualpa who stopped them, grabbing Simon by the arm, and pulling him back. 'There. On the path ahead. Just for a moment the smoke cleared and I could see something. There!'

Coughing and blinking, Simon and Bogart also saw something. It looked like two long tree trunks, with the branches blackened and scorched. The smoke was coming from the wood, billowing and curling towards them.

Bogart stepped forwards. 'Logs of wood. It's a trap that drops burning logs on top of you. Come on. They've sprung it already.'

All three of them began to walk towards the charred hunks of wood, when Simon stopped.

'If they're wood, why do they smell of ...? Look out!! Get back!!!'

His yell was too late.

A sheet of bright golden flame seared across the passage, right in front of them, burning with an intolerable heat.

Simon felt the skin blistering on his face and smelled his hair burning. Only at that moment did he recall the last words of Aenghs.

He had said : 'What a warm welcome they will get down there.'

Pain caught him by the throat, and he heard himself screaming.

His eyes burned with that ochre light.

It blazed into his mind.

The gold light softened and gradually became darker. Finally became black.

As abruptly as it had begun, the flame vanished, and the corridor was quiet again.

EIGHT

A Little Memento

The flash of flame as the sun broke through the lowering clouds made Simon wince. The dying Ahmed was nearly on top of him, and he could actually feel warm blood pattering on his face. High above him, just over the lip of the cliff, he could see Bogart starting to climb towards him, and there were other faces lining the edge, like a row of grapes on top of a wall.

Ahmed slid by him, missing him by a narrow margin of less than a metre. In a fraction of a second he would splash into the polluted liquid of the lake, and Simon turned his head slightly to one side so that he could watch.

The pain in his head had gone as quickly as it had arrived, and he realised that he was going to live. Not for the first time, he luxuriated in the feeling that death had brushed him with her wings – and passed on by.

'I felt the wings of the angel of death that time,' said Simon, climbing painfully to his feet. To either side of him, Bogie and Hualpa were also getting up.

Just as the jet of flame gushed out of the crevices in the rock, tripped by the fall of their feet on a certain stone, the pieces of the jigsaw had clicked together in Simon's brain, and he had seen the nature of the trap.

Aengh's words about a 'warm welcome'. The smell of burning flesh that they'd noticed. The short scream. The odd heat in the air. The smudges on the floor and walls. And the burned logs.

That weren't logs.

Hualpa peered through the shimmering air at the bodies, smouldering anew after the last gush of fire. With their new knowledge, it was possible to see where the charred arms and legs lay. Where the black ball that had once been a head hung on the floor. Trace the lines of the chest and trunk. Even spot the whiteness of protruding bone through the incinerated flesh.

'That is a heavy price to pay for their sins,' he said, his voice low.

'They're Erlik and Halda?' asked Bogart, though the question was really superfluous. Since there was no evidence of the remains of an exo, it couldn't be the thinker. And both corpses were normal size. So Corman and Fara had escaped.

'Yes. There wouldn't be any other of my people down here. It's proscribed. Aenghs is revenged.'

'No. He suffered for a long time. That was too quick a death for scum like that.'

Bogie was amazed at the cold hatred in Simon's voice, quite unlike the boy's normal friendly tones. He supposed that the torture of the old man had caused the change, but he was only partly right.

As they moved on, carefully testing their steps, they passed the remains of the traitors, now cooling. Casually Bogart spat on what was left of Erlik and Halda. 'Teaches you a lesson. Doesn't it?'

'What's that?' asked Hualpa.'

'Play with fire and you get your fingers burned,' said Bogart, laconically.

Silently, they padded on, deeper into the bowels of the mountain. Simon dimmed his lamp to the barest minimum, ready in case of a surprise attack. But their enemies were too busy to think of possible pursuers.

'Be careful, down here,' whispered Hualpa. 'They say

that the rocks are in a state of balance, and may crash down at any moment. It has been a worry of our community for generations that the cavern would collapse and our treasures and the atica buried.'

Boggart stopped at that and peered at the arty through the gloom. Amazement sparked out of every word. 'Then why don't you move it all to a safer place?'

Hualpa answered him, obviously surprised at the foolishness of the question : 'It has always been so.'

Bogart's reply trembled on the edge of his lips, but was checked by Simon holding up a cautionary finger. There was a light ahead of them, and they could hear voices. One thin and piping. The other deep and slow.

'They are in the cavern! They are actually in the cavern where the atica and everything are.' There was a bitter note of anguish in the arty's voice.

He began to move forward, as though impelled by some uncontrollable urge. Simon put his hand on his shoulder to try and check him, but he turned on him, teeth bared, snarling viciously. His fist struck out at Simon, sending him staggering back into Bogart, knocking him off balance. By the time they'd recovered, Hualpa was running full-pelt down the corridor, shouting at the top of his voice.

'Sacrilege! Blasphemy!! Treachery!!!'

Simon's bow had been wrecked when they fell over by the fire-trap, but Bogie managed to get his to his shoulder and aim at the back of the fleeing man.

'No, Bogie. Let's follow him. He may set up a play for us. We need a break.'

So, as quickly and quietly as possible, they followed Hualpa into the chamber, pausing just in the well of shadow near the entrance. Wondering at the bizarre tableau they saw there.

First, the protagonists. Waving his blaster menacingly stood Hualpa, his body streaked with sweat.

Facing him, a giant in nearly every way, was the towering figure of Fara, leader of the thinkers. His exo was different from that worn by the scientist they'd killed out in the back-lands. It was vastly heavier, and armoured round his puny body, with stronger struts at arm and leg.

All that was visible was the face, helmeted and goggled. The eyes, glazed and incurious behind thick lenses, were watching the arty.

Against the wall, gross and monstrous, like some huge spider in human form, Harley Corman also watched, a vaguely amused smile playing round his thick lips.

Those were the people.

But what gripped the eyes of Simon and Bogart were the contents of the room. Its vastness receding into the flicker-ing shadows, it seemed roughly circular. Perhaps fifty metres across. The walls, rough-hewn, rose in tiers to a height that they could only guess at as they were shrouded in black-ness.

And on the shelves! Simon gasped at the beauty and wonder of it all. Out of the corner of his eye, he saw Bogie's jaw drop.

There were paintings and sculptures. Flashing jewels and rich fabrics. Tapestries and figurines. Abstract shapes in gleaming chromes and golds, smooth and polished. Rough statues with pitted skins, each pore bearing a precious gem.

Simon knew virtually nothing of the value of works of art, but even he could appreciate the richness of that hoard. It truly was worth the ransom of a galaxy. If it were sold in small lots throughout the inhabited worlds it would pos-sibly realise more than the whole worth of Zayin. And it lay open to the greatest thief – Harley Corman.

Unless they could stop him.

Ahmed's body splashed into the lake, spraying bitter liquid

over Simon. It never came back to the surface. Just a few sullen bubbles disturbed the scummy surface.

'Ah. What a pleasant and unexpected surprise. I believe the name is Hualpa, is it not?'

The arty turned to look at Corman, disturbed by the man's incredible self-possession. 'You know me!' he screamed. 'And I know you! Your treachery has ruined Xoachtl and broken my people.'

Gently, as though waving away a troublesome insect on a summery day, Corman admonished the frantic man. 'Please. A little less volume. I am reliably informed that this cavern is not of the safest. It would be a shame to lose all this beauty. Not to mention the only supply of atica in the universe.'

For the first time Simon was aware of the priceless drug, glowing with a soft light in a corner of the room. Attached to an unusual rock formation, it was a small heap of a light green powder. Perhaps forty or fifty kilos. If that.

The arty brought his voice under control, aware that a fine dust of sand was dropping from the vaulted roof of the chamber. Fallen stones scattered over the floor and near the walls were a mute testimony to the danger they were all in.

'It is not just my people who are destroyed. You, thinker! You will count your dead in tens and hundreds. If you take Xoachtl, your victory will cost you all.'

Slowly the head of Fara swivelled to gaze at Corman. 'What does he mean by that? You told me, and I told all my colleagues, that things would be made easier by your treachery here. That we would take the fortress with only minimal losses. Is that not so?'

Corman stepped forward a couple of paces, his hands in the pockets of his crumpled trousers. 'Now, now, Fara, my old companion. If I were pressed for an answer, I could only say that my expectations were not totally fulfilled. The arties here have evidently shown greater courage and resistance than I had estimated they would. I can only . . .'

Angered beyond any restraint, Hualpa squeezed the firing button of his blaster, the stream of energy narrowly missing Corman and splattering a chunk of rock from the wall. There was a creaking, and more small stones showered down over all of them.

'You murdering, torturing bastard ! ! ! There is nobody that you keep your word with.'

Gently, as though reproaching a naughty grandchild, Corman answered him. 'Aaah. Now there you are wrong. And, please, have more care where you point that toy. I wouldn't wish to end my days as an incinerated lump of charcoal. Or buried beneath miles of falling rock. Where was I? Yes; you say that I am not honest with anyone. That is a falsehood. My old tutor, the late and much lamented Casper Gutman, once told me to be true to myself. And to no one else. I have followed his teachings as well as I could.'

The thinker was not satisfied and moved closer, the head swivelling to watch both Hualpa and Corman. Hidden in the darkness, Simon and Bogart watched silently and helplessly. Bogie had one of his last couple of arrows ready, but the distance was great and the light uncertain. All they could do was watch and wait.

'Corman. Does this man speak the truth?'

Testily, the fat man answered : 'I don't know. If he says that his people and yours are being wiped out then he probably knows what he's talking about.'

The arty took another step towards them, the blaster pointed at Corman. 'Listen, thinker. This man has fooled us all. He doesn't care for us or for you. Ask him what he truly wants. Ask him about the treasures he wants to keep for himself. And ask him about the atica. Why don't you do . . .'

His voice was cut off as sharply as a bolt of lightning. The fat man had a tiny palm weapon concealed up his sleeve, and had decided that it was time to use it. His aim was quite impeccable.

The arty flung his arms up above his head, the blaster bouncing metallically off the wall, clipping a fine old porcelain statue as it fell to lie in the sand. A small hole had been drilled in his head, just below the right eye and close to the nose. There was another hole just behind the left ear and nearly level with the top of it.

If it hadn't been for the flooding of blood and brains, it would have been theoretically possible to see clean through the hole in the head. It killed Hualpa instantly.

It all happened between heartbeats, and neither Simon nor Bogart moved. One of the exo's hands flicked at a blurring speed, and a needle laser extended towards the fat man.

The voice of the thinker cracked out. 'Do not try that trick with me, Corman. I will kill you as soon as look at you. Before you die, I am curious to know if what that relic said was true.'

Shrugging his massive shoulders, Corman bowed his head penitently. 'Mea culpa, Fara. Mea maxima culpa. I can only admit that there is more than a little truth in his infamous last words. Yes. I want the treasures. And, yes, I want the rest of the atica. But, most of all, yes, I underestimated the resistance of the arties here. I hoped they'd tie you and your people up for a time while I helped myself to a small bonus. However . . .' The sentence dangled off into a musing silence.

'Very well.' Fara held the control panel for his exo ready at his chest. His short arms, ending in feeble fingers, were hidden by the massive armour. His back was turned to the entrance to the chamber. All around him, unwinking spectators of the bizarre scene, were the collected artworks of generations of some of the finest painters and sculptors the universe had ever known. And, over it all, the fine dust rained down, squeezed by unimaginable pressures to the consistency of water.

'Fara. Is it no use appealing to your tiny and limited brain to offer you a full half share in all this?' Expansively, the fat man waved his arms round the cavern. 'Think of it. With the treasures alone we could be the richest men in the galaxy. With the last supplies of atica, there would be no man and no union that could hope to stand against us.'

'Blood offerings!' The voice was amplified by the exo and echoed shrilly about them. There was a creaking and a heavy thud as a larger boulder slipped out of place. Neither man seemed aware of it.

'Simon. I once read an old book about this crazy man who thought he'd buried his sister alive. They lived in an ancient house that was falling down. In the end it fell in a river and they were all killed. Let's get out of here before those two lunatics bring all this down on them and us. Come on.'

But Simon couldn't move. He knew that there was a lot of sense in what Bogie said, but he couldn't tear himself away from the drama winding to its close right in front of him.

'Blood offerings!!' repeated the thinker, swinging his enormously powerful arms in the air in his rage. 'Corman!! How . . . you have killed and tortured men and women here.'

'No, no, Fara. I cannot possibly allow you to say that without defending myself. I have personally done little of that. Much of the worst things have come about through stupid or over-enthusiastic subordinates of mine.'

'You equivocate overlong. Not only have you ruined our plans for conquest of Zayin, you have managed to wipe out my people.'

'Tut, tut. Is there no gratitude left in this backworld galaxy? You forget that your enemies, the arties, also appear to have been destroyed.'

Bitter though his hatred was for what Corman had manipulated, Simon couldn't help a faint, sneaking feeling of respect for the class the man was showing when faced with the certainty of death.

Behind his mask, the thinker seemed to be in danger of having a fit. It was some seconds before the squeaks and splutters subsided enough for them to make out the words.

'That is all I will hear. After your death, I will take the atica for myself. I will benefit from your wickedness. Not you. Die!'

As he spat out the last words, Simon wordlessly reached out and took the bow and makeshift arrow from Bogie's fingers. The thinker raised his powerful prosthetic arm, pointing it at the fat man, who made no move to dodge his destiny. At that moment Simon drew the string back to his nose, sighting along the jagged pointed steel, and loosed.

There was the faintest thunk of the string releasing its energy. Simon drew his breath in as it nipped him painfully on the inside of his left forearm. He'd aimed at the only visible and vulnerable part of the thinker – his face. All the rest was safe behind protecting armour.

From the moment he loosed, and saw the shaft fly gleaming through the dimness, he knew what would happen.

He'd missed.

Commander Rack sat up, wiping the stinking liquid from his stained uniform, knowing that the acids in it would burn holes within the hour. Looking vaguely round for his colt and not being able to see it. Grinning up as he heard cursing from his colleague who was sliding down the face of the bluff to help him.

His head felt like a still pool after a pebble's been lobbed into the middle of it. The ripples were just beginning to finally subside.

The shaft flew low, Simon's eye deceived by the size of the

cavern and the poor lighting. It struck home about half a metre below Fara's head, cracking against the delicate control panel, splintering and bursting it.

For a moment the thinker clearly didn't realise what had happened. He still tried to kill Corman. There was a faint hissing and a glow of purple light from the exo's controls, and the left arm twitched convulsively.

'What's happening? What have you done? I've been shot by someone! ! ! !'

The last word rose to a piercing scream, as the exoskeleton began to move. Obviously without Fara's guidance. In front of it, Corman showed little surprise at the last-second rescue, merely peering into the shadows where Simon and Bogart stood. The arrow had bounced off the exo to land near his feet. To pick it up was obviously hard for a man of Corman's girth, and he contented himself with staring down at it, and then looking again to the blackness.

'Corman! ! Quickly. Help me. It's out of . . . Aaaaaa-aaah! ! !'

There was a grating of gears, and sparks shot out of the front of the vast aid. Like a giant bearing a child on its shoulders, the exo took huge steps. First to the right, and then to the left. The macabre dance ended as suddenly as it had begun, when it began to swing round, pivoting on its durstel heels, the arms beginning to revolve like manic windmills.

A stream of fire shot out of the end of one hand, exploding against the weak roof. Molten rock dripped over the tiers of treasure, washing a series of ancient sonic sculptures to instant, mute destruction. Tapestries flared drily in the heat, setting fire to paintings and plastic forms.

Moving unexpectedly fast for such a gross man, Corman dodged lightly away from the raging behemoth and skipped to the pile of atica, kneeling down in it and scraping up handfuls into the capacious pockets of his suit.

For the first time Simon shouted to him. 'Harley Corman!! Come out of there.'

Without looking back, contenting himself with keeping one eye on the dervish exoskeleton, Corman continued to try and fill his hands with the priceless dust. 'I somehow knew that you were my knight in shining armour defeating this nasty little dragon. Though, I'm no unsullied maiden for you to keep as a prize.'

'Get out! The roof's coming in!!'

The exo still whirled, shaking its top half violently to and fro. There was no more sound from the thinker, who was obviously having to devote all his puny strength to hanging on. If he hadn't been so tightly strapped in, Fara would have been hurled to his doom against the crumbling rocks.

Grunting with the effort, Corman heaved off his jacket, tying the arms together to make a sort of sack. Cautiously, Simon and Bogie stepped in, dodging the falling pebbles as best they could. Catching at Simon's arm, Bogie shouted: 'It's no use. Let the stupid bastard kill himself. It's coming in like I said. Like that book. Come on.'

The exo was extending and shortening its arms and legs with frightening speed, swirling them through the air, and still revolving. All the various aids and weapons were being used at random. Flames hissed through the dusty air, and jets of poisonous fluids pattered off the treasures.

Corman had finally filled his coat with enough atica to fetch a galaxy's ransom, when he saw Simon coming for him. Mouth working, he backed away.

'No. My dear boy, I'll cut you and your chum in for equal shares. Come now. Surely we can agree to differ. Forget past differences. Forget all acrimony. Don't despise an old...'

His semi-literary wanderings were brutally cut off. The exo, its chest glowing a fiery red, staggered his way, and one of the arms clubbed out at Corman. It caught him in the centre of the back, with gigantic force. The fat man was completely lifted off his feet by the impact, and his precious bundle of atica went flying into a corner, where it burst into a phosphorescent cloud.

Corman was flung into the opposite corner, furthest away from the entrance, where he lay like a monstrous doll, discarded by a wilful child. More stones and rocks were falling now, and it was becoming hard to see across the chamber.

Simon stopped dead, watching the exo warily. Bogart was at his shoulder, eyes lit up with the mad joy of action, dodging a scything cut from a metallic arm. It was hard to know if the thinker was still alive or not, but his body was still strapped in place atop the flailing robot aid.

'Look out!' yelled Bogie, as the exo began new and more violent movements. Like a durstel battering ram, it suddenly lowered its top half and rushed at the wall. There was a sickening squelching crack as the remains of the scientist were pulped into the sandy rock face. All that was left on the wall was a dark stain, flecked with grey and white. Again and again the exo launched itself against the rock, its arms beating at the ceiling, and its legs kicking maniacally at the tiers of treasure.

Wonderful crystal flowers were demolished into shards of gleaming glass. Paintings, the colours as fresh as when they were produced centuries ago, vanished into strips of torn canvas. Gold and silver were laid in the dust in twisted lumps. Flames blossomed from some of the shelves and melting metal dribbled across the floor, cooling in dull pools around the rocks.

There was a sickly crack from somewhere deep within the exo and it became instantly still. One arm swung slowly down like an unwinding pendulum. Its top half was mangled beyond recognition, and there was nothing visible of the flattened corpse of Fara, leader of the thinkers.

With a rumbling like a starship docking in a ravine of steel, a gigantic boulder was loosened from the ceiling and dropped with ponderous slowness to shake the floor with its fall. Others followed it, and the whole chamber was quivering with strain.

Simon's brain reeled as he saw the mighty walls rushing asunder, and his ears burst at the noise of the rocks grinding apart. With Bogart panting at his heels, he ran for his life from that cavern, where huge stones rained down, burying for all time the greatest treasure house in the galaxy. And the most powerful drug ever known.

They raced up tottering corridors, retracing their steps. Hurdled the burned bodies of the traitors, onwards and upwards towards clean air and light. While they ran, there was a rushing of wind at their heels, and a massive explosion deep behind them. Sand stung their backs, and then there was quiet.

A few distant settlings, and then a deep silence.

Both stopped in their tracks, heads down, panting for breath, feeling their lungs near to bursting. Simon dropped to his heels, leaning against the cool rock.

'That's it, then.'

'Yes. That's it. Nobody's going back there again. Not ever. Eh?'

Simon coughed, hawking up sand. 'All we've got to do now is avoid being killed by any arties or thinkers left alive, and trek back to Fort Peine. Make sure we don't get busted for those killings. Wait for the *Venturer* and try to explain why we're not really deserters.'

Bogie laughed. 'That's okay. No problem for a couple of willing lads like us. Seriously though, I reckon we might do all right back at GalSec for what we've done.'

'What's that? Both sects are ended. No chance for either of them now all that lot's gone. So. Probably means the whole world's doomed to extinction. Is that what we've done?'

They began to walk slowly back, both feeling the dullness of anticlimax. Recognising the pains they'd been able to ignore while the adrenalin pumped through their bodies.

'There's no point thinking that, Simon. If you see two nutters attacking each other and you try to stop it, it can't be helped if you don't manage and they kill each other. You've saved them hurting anyone else, and that's something. Isn't it?'

There was no answer. 'Well, isn't it?'

'I suppose so, Bogie.'

'Right. And the atica's safe. And we won't see any more of that fat bastard Corman.'

'I'm not so sure, Bogie.'

Bogart stopped so abruptly that Simon stumbled over his heels. 'What d'you mean? You're not sure! Come on, Simon. Ain't nobody getting out from under that. Anyway, that exo spread him all over the walls.'

'No.'

'No!'

'No. I reckon that if he'd been normal size, he'd have had his bones cracked to splinters. But because he's so fat I reckon it cushioned him.'

They were getting closer to the surface, and the air seemed cleaner.

Bogart paused to rub a bruised knee. 'I mean . . . if he'd been alive, then he'd have been moving. Wouldn't he?'

'That's just it. When the exo ran amok, smashing everything up, just before that frigging huge rock dropped down, the sand and smoke cleared for a second, and I saw Corman quite distinctly. His head was raised and he was half up. On his hands and knees. It was odd really. What a queer man he was. Or is. You can't help having a kind of grudging admiration for him.'

'Why? What did he do?'

Simon grinned reminiscently. 'Well, remember that all his plans were in tatters. When I saw him he noticed me watching him at the same second. Our eyes met. So I know he's alive.'

'What'd he do?'
'Winked.'

The top levels of Xoachtl were devastated. Bodies lay everywhere and the morning air was heavy with the sweet cloying odour of death. Smoke still wreathed sullenly about the Water Gate.

The fight in the council chamber had continued with fierce determination on both sides. The main doorway was completely blocked with mangled corpses and Simon and Bogart had to make their way out by side turnings. Few of the survivors were without wounds. The moaning of the dying hung about the fortress and the passages were sticky with blood.

It was hard to calculate the losses. The remaining thinkers had left, knowing the battle was not won. Even though it had not truly been lost. The remaining arties were wandering about the rooms in a state of shock.

One or two challenged Simon and he told them most of what had happened. But not about the total loss of their treasures and the atica.

'They've had enough for one day, Bogie. If they found out now about that they'd all just curl up and die.'

At a guess Simon reckoned that the thinkers had lost between one hundred and fifty and two hundred dead or severely wounded. The arties' losses seemed to have been nearly double that. But they had lacked the powerful armoured exos of the scientists. And there had been many more of them in the first place.

So it went.

There were several of the thinkers' floaters left lying around the ruins of Xoachtl, and they took one each to get them back to Fort Peine. Using the fortress's communications centre, they had managed to contact the *Venturer*, giving a concise outline of what had been happening. In an unexcited voice the operator had passed on the news that the starship would be returning to Fort Peine within forty-eight hours, and that instructions would be passed to the civil authorities to expect Ensign Bogart and Midman Rack and hold them safely pending an investigation into their story.

They'd taken protective clothing from the arties to keep the blazing sun from baking them again. Water and food for their inner needs and soothing unguents for their cuts and bruises. There was still about two hours of light left.

Out in the backlands Simon throttled back on his floater and gently revolved to look back at the mountain. There were still the bright blobs of a few sirques dotted about the orange cliffs, but most had been destroyed in the fighting or by the retreating thinkers out of spite.

Heavy smoke circled and coiled lazily out of the holes in the fortress, marking the funeral pyre of a whole people. High above Xoachtl, glittering so brightly that it hurt to look on it, the Eye still shone. Open. Unseeing. Blank and blind. An empty symbol.

Bogart stopped a few metres away and looked at the mighty ruin in silence.

'Well, young Simon Rack. I reckon that's the end.'

Turning so that his back was to Xoachtl, Simon shook his head. 'No, Bogie. As far as we're concerned, I think that it's just a beginning.'

With which epic and prophetic thought they continued on their way across the desert under the setting sun.

NINE

Meanwhile ...

Small pebbles dimpled the surface of the stinking pool as Bogart slid down to meet him. Feeling distinctly shaky round the knees, Simon stood up and faced him. With a final rush the ensign was with him, coming within an ace of toppling right forward into the lake.

'You're all right, Simon?'

'I'm kay. More than we can say for Ahmed. He's under there somewhere. Sinking slowly in the mess.'

Bogart grinned at him. 'Can't say I'll shed many tears for him. Nearly did for you. Still, I got him right. Full kill on the colt. He didn't hear me creeping up behind him. Just standing there watching you on the way down. The sod didn't say anything. Just sniffed. Then I hit him.'

Together they started the long, long climb back up to the row of watching men and women on the crest of the hill. Just for a moment Simon paused and shook his head, trying to clear the last wisps of the mind-scrambler.

'What did that odd gun of his do to you, anyway?'

'Well . . .' he wondered whether it had really happened as he remembered it. 'I'll tell you about it some other time, Bogie. It wasn't exactly *all* my past life that flashed by as I was falling. Just a few cherished memories. Don't worry. I'll tell you about them later on. Quite interesting.'

As they neared the top, Simon looked up and saw all the top brass of the secret weapons establishment waiting impatiently to hear from him what had happened.

Bogart patted him cheerfully on the back. The smell of the ammonia lake had gradually diminished, until they were hardly aware of it any more.

'That's it, then. Another happy ending.'

Simon stopped, holding on to a tussock of coarse grass to keep his balance. Far below him the corpse of Ahmed had just reached the silted bottom of the thick soup-like liquid, the secret weapon already beginning to erode in the corrosive liquid.

'Sorry, Bogie. What'd you say?'

'I just said that this was another of our famous happy endings.'

'You know what? The older I get, the more I realise that there aren't really any happy endings. Not in our job. Just lots of beginnings.'

'Come on. There's got to be an ending somewhere, Simon. Hasn't there?'

'Yes. Death.'

For a moment the sun broke through the heavy clouds and bathed the hillside in a pale golden light.